Love is a Long Journey

Day 1

A disparate group gathered in the hotel lobby for the 10 o'clock group meeting. They differed in age, gender, race and religion but they all had one thing in common. They were going on an adventure.

An attractive woman in her mid twenties sat quietly on the brown leather sofa. Her hair cascaded down her shoulders and she was slim and stylish. Her polar opposite plonked herself next to her. Nancy was a plump, warm and friendly American in her early thirties. "Geeze, I'm excited about this," she exclaimed. "I'm Nancy, pleased to meet you."
"Hi," said Florence, clearly not wanting to chat.

David, the charismatic group leader began by introducing himself. He was 37 years old and a confirmed nomad. He'd been leading tours for the company across the globe and claimed to have had many rich experiences. "You've all got a folder containing a copy of the itinerary which I'll go through and it tells you who your roommate will be if you haven't paid the single supplement. If you want to swap during the tour, that is fine. Just negotiate between yourselves and let me know if you switch. You've got the rest of the day to explore the town and settle in. We'll meet back here at 8 am tomorrow. We have a one-hour drive to the start of our four-day hike.

Pack a small day pack. The support vehicle will take the rest of your luggage and the tents but everyone will need to muck in to pitch tents and prepare food."

David talked through the salient points of the itinerary and then took questions.

"Can we have details on the rock climbing?' asked a tall and handsome young man called Oliver.
"Yes, of course. Where there are locations where rock climbing is offered on the itinerary you will be able to pay locally. All equipment is included and it is suitable for beginners."
"And if you are advanced? Are there locations that are challenging?"
"Oh, yes," replied David. "In most locations there are routes that are ideal for advanced rock climbers. Don't worry, Olly, I'll make sure I hook you up with the right instructor."
"Thanks," replied Oliver.

"Oh, who is he?" whispered Nancy to Florence. "He's gorgeous! What do you think, Flo?"
"Not my type. Far too plummy."
"Come again?"
'Private school type. Sense of entitlement oozes out of him, if you ask me."
"Sorry, you've lost me," said Nancy.
"Oh, it's an English thing. You don't have types like him in America and lucky you."

"I hope he's my roommate!" said Nancy, searching in her folder. "Oh, it looks as if you and I are sharing Florence."
"Sorry to disappoint," said Florence, sarcastically.
"You'll do, Honey!" said Nancy jokingly. "Don't worry. I plan on getting a seat next to him on the bus so I can snooze on his shoulder."
"You go for it," said Florence, sounding thoroughly bored. "But keep me out of it. I don't want to be in your romantic movie".
"Those pecks could have a starring role," said Nancy, dreamily.
Florence grabbed her bag and walked off, looking exasperated, towards the rooms to settle in.

Mohammed, a cheerful man from England approached Oliver. "Hi Mate, I think you've pulled the short straw."
Oliver looked confused. "We're sharing a room."
"Oh, said Oliver. "Great! Do you snore?"
"I don't think so. You?"
"No, but I've got smelly feet!"
"Well, keep them well away from me," laughed Mohammed. "Let's find the room, Mate."

Some of the group gathered in the bar after dinner for a drink. They met as strangers about to embark on a long road trip that would inevitably put them in situations where they would get to know each other very well. Mohammed joined them in a Luton Town Football shirt.

"Luton Town? You sure you want to admit to that Mate? You could probably get arrested for that around here," said Nick, a short stocky man in his late twenties.
"Yer, very funny, Nick! Who do you support?"
Nick pulled up his jumper to reveal a West Ham shirt.
"Not surprised you want to keep that one hidden," said Mohammed, clearly pulling his leg.
"How about you, Olly?" said Nick. "Who do you support?"
"I don't really support anyone, Southampton if you push me," replied Oliver.
"He's probably a rugby and cricket fan," said Florence.
"How did you know that?" asked Oliver, with a quizzical look on his face.
"Oh, it's not rocket science," said Florence cryptically. "It's going to be a long day tomorrow. I think, I'll go to bed." With that she got up and left.

Nancy stayed in the bar for longer but when she got back to the room she found Florence sat up in bed reading.
"I'm curious," she said. "How did you know Olly was a cricket and rugby fan?"
"Simple," she said. "He's posh."
"I'm sorry," replied Nancy, looking very confused. "You need to explain that to me."
"Nick and Mo are from working class back grounds. I know Nick is a lawyer but his roots are clearly working class. He probably, like Mo, and me for that

matter, went to a comprehensive school so they would have played football and supported their local teams. Oliver, on the other hand, went to a private school where they had a pavilion, and played rugby and cricket with cucumber sandwiches at half time."
"Are private schools expensive?" asked Nancy
"Try £10,000 a term!" laughed Florence.
"Wow!" said Nancy, looking shocked.

Day 2

The next morning the sky was a brilliant blue and the town, fringed by jagged mountains, was sparkling. When Florence boarded the bus she noticed that Nancy was sat next to Oliver, chatting to him and looking very animated. Florence moved towards the back of the bus and sat next to Akemi from Japan. Akemi spoke some English but was not fluent so they showed each other photos on their phone to help keep the conversation going.

The trail began by following a narrow fast flowing river. It wasn't particularly steep but it was uneven with loose stones making it more treacherous. Shepherds looked on from a distance but their dogs barked loudly and sometimes snarled as if to warn the group to beware.

'It's a hard life,' said David. These guys stay out stay here for weeks on end, far removed from the comforts of civilisation. And that is in all winds and weathers.

If they get hit by a snow storm then it can be fatal, not just for their sheep but for them too."
"So you can't order a pizza?" asked Mohammed, jokingly.
"No!" replied David. They have no communication with the outside world."
"None!" said Mohammed, looking incredulous!
"No, none!" laughed David.
"I won't be applying to be a shepherd any time soon!" replied Mohammed, emphatically.
"Life's not one long social media orgy!" said Florence sternly. "They have this beautiful eco-system for their office."
"Quite right!" smiled David. "It does have its advantages."

As the day went on, the group started to spread out. Mohammed and Oliver headed the group but Nancy lagged at the back.
"You're in the dog house!" said Oliver to Mohammed.
"What Mate?"
"With old Flossy Flo!"
"Oh yer! *They have this beautiful eco-system for their office!*' he trilled, imitating Florence very well, but he looked over his shoulder to check she was nowhere near and to reassure himself that he hadn't been over heard.
"Ohhhh, you scared of her?"
"Too right I am!" replied Mohammed. "She'd eat me for breakfast. Mind you, I might go for that option!"
"You nymphomaniac!" laughed Oliver.

After six hours walking, muscles were aching and back packs seemed heavier. During the afternoon they had climbed higher up the valley. They were relieved to see the equipment that had been dropped in a sheltered hollow by the support team. David was soon barking orders to ensure tents were erected and dinner organised before it got dark. With dinner quickly demolished the group sat round a roaring fire and relaxed after a long first day.

"Where did all those stars come from? They don't have stars like that in London," observed Nick.

"Don't they?" asked Nancy.

"No, too much light pollution."

"Too much pollution of every kind!" added Florence. "It is very refreshing to be somewhere with clean air."

"Yes," said David but even this pristine environment doesn't escape from the ravages of climate change. The glaciers in the area, for example, are receding."

"It makes me so angry," said Florence and is exactly why I joined the Extinction Rebellion Protests.

"Oh, it was you who stopped me getting across London!" joked Oliver.

Florence glared at him. "It's not a joke!" and with that she got up and went off to her tent.

"Wow! She's sensitive," said Nick.

"Well, in her defence," said David, "it is a serious issue and she's obviously passionate about fighting climate change. I get that."

"Yer, you're right," said Oliver, "It was a crass comment."

"Easily done, Mate but if you don't want to end up being hit over the head with her placard, I'd tread carefully in future!"

Most members of the group drifted off to bed but Oliver, Mohammed and Nick stayed around the dying embers drinking beer. "This reminds me of camping as a kid in the Peak District," said Mohammed. "You're lucky," said Nick. "We never went on holiday. My Old Man thought they were a waste of money. I guess I'm making up for lost time now!"
"How about you, Oliver?"
"Camping!"
"Yer right!" exclaimed Mohammed. "Was that on safari in Kenya?"
"Oh, ok," said Oliver, "but don't tell Flossy! She won't be impressed by the air miles! I did do some conservation work with orangutans in Borneo but somehow, I don't think that will impress her either!"

So you've never been abroad before this then, Nick?" asked Mohammed.
"No, not really. I did go to a friend's stag do in Amsterdam for a weekend. Does that count?"
"Yes! Did you shag all weekend in the Red Light District and smoke dope? Sounds like my ideal weekend."
"No, Mo, we didn't! We had a few beers by a canal and went for a Chinese!"
"Well that's boring!"

"Well most of us do lead boring lives. It's not all one glamorous vlog as you'd like it to be. Most of us that were on the trip are in the legal profession so it was never going to be Amsterdam on speed."
"So no one got drunk and fell in a canal?"
"No! We did see a few nude women."
"Oh, now you're talking!" said Mohammed, his interest revived.
"Yes, at an art gallery."
"You went to an art gallery on a stag weekend? Oh, that's really sad!"

"How about you, Mo? Have you been on any shag filled trips then?"
"No," said Mohammed. "My mates and I planned one in Faliraki for the summer after I did my A Levels but my dad got wind of it from one of the other parents and my mum hid my passport. The worse bit was the lads went without me and had a great time. They were drunk all week and sent me photos of their conquests."

"It's a shame human communities aren't more like bonobo communities," said Oliver.
"What?" said Nick and Mohammed in unison.
"What the hell has this got to do with the tragedy of me missing out on a right of passage?"
"Well bonobos are monkeys that spend most of their time having sex."
"Oh, now you're talking!" said Mohammed.
"Yes, I assumed you'd approve, Mo," laughed Oliver.
"They make love not war so they are never aggressive.

In most primate societies females are marginalised but in bonobo society they are equal and central within the troupe."

"I think I'd rather be one of those baboons who leads a troupe. They were in the latest David Attenborough wildlife documentary," mused Mohammed.

"Why?" asked Nick.

"Well obviously because you get to have sex with every female in the troupe, and you get exclusive rights!"

"Yer, but you have to keep fighting off all those randy males who want to have sex with your females," said Oliver.

"Bring it on is what I say!" said Mohammed.

"Yer, you definitely make a good Alpha Male!" laughed Oliver.

Florence found it hard to find her tent in the dark, in spite of having a small torch and she was still seething about Oliver's earlier comment. She could hear the boys laughing down by the campfire and imagined that they were talking about her. Losing concentration, she tripped over a rock and fell awkwardly. "Oh, that man!" she thought, mentally blaming Oliver.

Day 3

Florence's ankle swelled up by the morning and made walking painful. David gave her a thick bandage from the first aid box and advised her to bind it tightly.

"Have you taken pain killers?" he asked.

"Yes" replied Florence, "but they haven't done much good yet."
"Do you want to stay in the support van today?"
Florence paused, "Not really. How far is it today?"
"We'll be walking for approximately six hours but you could join the support van after two hours as there is a road where they could drive and meet us. I can radio them if that's what you want to do."
"Yes, that sounds good. Thanks, David."
"The first part is a gentle incline but it does get steeper later on. Just let me know what to do about half eleven and I'll sort that out."

Unusually, Florence stuck with Nancy at the back of the group. Nancy tried to raise her spirits with a few jokes and a bit of gossip about the starry eyed couple who rarely engaged with the rest of the group, oblivious to much outside their own sphere of being. Florence, however, was quiet and lost in her own thoughts. "You seem very down today," observed Nancy.
"Yes, I'm feeling a bit homesick but I'm just tired and my ankle injury doesn't help.
"Well soon we've got three nights in a hotel so you'll be able to rest and catch your breath. You'll be fine, kid."
"Yer, I know! Thanks for the pep talk, Nancy!"

Up ahead they saw Oliver sat on a rock looking at them as they approached.

"Can I carry your ruck sack?" asked Oliver. "It might relieve the pressure on your ankle."

"No thanks," replied Florence brusquely and quickened her pace.

Nancy, who had observed this exchange, noticed that Oliver looked momentarily crest fallen but recovered quickly and was soon back at the head of the group, chatting to David.

"Why did you do that?" she said, frowning at Florence. "I'd kill for him to carry my bag!"

"Oh, he was just being patronising," replied Florence, looking irritated.

"No he wasn't! He knows you twisted your ankle and just wanted to help. He's a nice guy. You just need to give him a break!"

"If he was a stick of rock, he'd have jerk written right through him."

"I could over look that," said Nancy, ruefully but he's never going to look at me. "You're in a different class though. I've seen him gazing at you."

"I'm sorry?" exclaimed, Florence. "Oh, you're mad, Nancy! Life isn't one long love story!"

"I repeat. He's a nice guy. You're too uptight for your own good."

"And don't use the word 'nice', you're better than that. I'm sure you've got a rich vocabulary hidden away in there, Nance!"

"Gracious, courteous, gallant, oh I know, chivalrous!!" joked Nancy.

"Oh shut up!" chuckled Florence.

Day 6

Sometime later, the group set out on a walk through a steep gorge. Trees clung precipitously to the towering cliffs that bordered it and bird song competed with the roar of a waterfall. Florence noticed that Nancy's ankle was bandaged and she was limping. Shortly afterwards she observed her pass her bag to Oliver who slung it on his own back and walked with her.

At lunch, she accosted Nancy. "When did you hurt your ankle?" she asked, looking sceptical.
"I slipped in the shower," replied Nancy with a twinkle in her eye.
"You didn't mention anything about that to me," said Florence.
"I'm not after sympathy," said Nancy in a mock heroic tone.
"No!" countered Florence. "Not from me, anyway!"
"Oh, I've had enough of your interrogation," laughed Nancy. "I'm going where I can get some sympathy!"
"Yer, I bet you are!" laughed Florence.

Later in the day, when Florence and Nancy were both relaxing on their beds, Florence reading and Nancy listening to music, Florence asked what she and Oliver had talked about.
"Oh, this and that!" smiled Nancy.
"What does 'this and that' mean?" asked Florence, sounding irritated.

"I don't remember specifics," said Nancy, "I just remember feeling very relaxed in his company."
"Um!" said Florence. "It sounds as if you were just looking starry eyed at him the whole time."
"Yep!" said Nancy, unashamedly.
"I bet he spent the whole time talking about himself!"
"No, not at all! He was more interested in me. He asked about my job, my family and the area where I live. He did mention his Mum and Dad who he seems close to and he's got a younger sister but he didn't tell me much. Oh, and he did say he'd had some mental health problems and been depressed for a few years but he didn't go in to any details and it's not the sort of thing you can ask about."
"What the hell has he got to be depressed about?" asked Florence, visibly bristling.
"Oh, you're so judgemental, Florence. You don't know the guy so you're hardly in a position to say that. I know if I said I'd been depressed you'd be sympathetic and supportive so I don't understand why you can't express some sympathy for him."
"Oh, it's probably not clinical depression, just fed up because he didn't get those top grades or that top job. People like him just expect everything to fall in to their laps!"
"Well, having spoken to him I wouldn't be too sure you're right, Flo," replied Nancy. "Anyway, tell me in more detail why you despise him so much."
"It's complicated," replied Florence.

"Oh my Lord!" smiled Nancy. "I don't get you Brits, you're so reserved. You need to be more like us brash, loud Americans!"
They both laughed and settled back to their previous activities.

Day 7

"Stop bloody filming me, Mo!" said Oliver. Looking up from his book on 'Alexander the Great'. He was stretched out on a sofa in the hotel lounge area.
"How many times do I have to tell you to piss off?"
"Oh, come on Mate! Have a heart! Every time I film you my 'likes' rocket."
"I don't give a damn! What don't you understand about 'I don't want to be in your stupid vlog'."
"Well when it goes viral you'll regret that decision. You could be scouted for 'Love Island'"
"Oh, I give up!" said Oliver, sounding exasperated.
"That is never going to happen!"
"You don't know!"
"Oh I do, because my Mum and sister would disown me."
"Why?" asked Mohammed.
"Well isn't that obvious?"
"No!" he replied, looking confused.
"Have you ever watched it?"
"Yes!"
"Well my Mum and sister are staunch feminists."
"I still don't get it!" said Mohammed, blankly.

"Oh, for goodness sake. Well obviously because it's demeaning towards women."
"Is it?"
"Yes, take it from me, it's sexist and misogynistic Mate."
"So your Mum would get on well with Flossy Flo then?" asked Mohammed.
"Oh, she's a light weight compared to my Mum."
"Oh and my dad and I are feminists too!"
"You what?" said Mohammed, pulling a face. "Men can't be feminists!"
"Yes they can! Andy Murray the tennis star is a feminist!"
"Is he? Is that because he's got that scary Mum. Is your Mum scary?"
"Yes, if you cross her," laughed Oliver.
"Well I think women should be seen and not heard! Know their place!" he joked.
"Why does that not surprise me?" laughed Oliver.
"Oh look out, incoming. Flossy Flo on the prowl!"

"What did you call me?" demanded Florence, only hearing his last comment.
"Flossy Flo," smiled Mo, sheepishly.
"Why?"
Mohammed became flustered, "It's your nick name. A term of endearment!"
"Oh is it! Well your nickname is Moron Mo and that is not a term of endearment." With that, she marched off.
"I think she just ate you alive, Mate!" said Oliver, falling off the sofa as he was laughing so much.

"She's a man hater, if you ask me! I bet she's got a mace spray and rape alarm in that ruck sack of hers. Don't get too close Olly or you'll find yourself blinded with a high pitched ringing in your ears!" said Mohammed.

"Don't worry Mate! I don't intend to get to get within 100 meters of her if I can help it! 100 miles would be better!"

Day 9

It had been a long hard slog up a rocky mountain and down the other side. Pulses were racing and sweat was pouring like rivers. As they scrabbled down the final stretch the men at the front found a swimming hole.

"Hey, Dave!" shouted Nick to their guide. "Is this safe to cool off in here?"

"Yes!" replied David, catching up with them but only jumping. It's not safe to dive in."

"Ok, dad!" laughed Oliver.

By the time the rest of the group caught up they had stripped to their boxer shorts.

"Oh, hello!" said Simon. Take a look at those pecks.

"Coming through!" exclaimed Nancy. "I need a ring side seat."

Oliver was the first to jump in making a loud splash, closely followed by Nick who screamed like a banshee and Obi.

Mohammed paused and looked nervously over the steep cliff to the dark water below. Florence, who observed from a distance, noticed his reticence. "Come on you wuss!" shouted Oliver, up to him. Mohammed continued to pause. "Get on with it!" Mohammed took a deep breath and jumped. The spectators cheered and Florence's eyes were fixed on him.

Shortly after entering the water Mohammed started to flail about. It was clear he was having a panic attack and struggling to stay afloat. He gasped for air. The other men in the water seemed unsure what to do for a split second but then Oliver, who was clearly a strong swimmer, swam over to him and grabbed him under both arms. "It's ok, Mo, I've got you. Just breath. I'll get you out of here."

Mohammed looked deathly white as Oliver swam backwards with him in his arms to the edge of the pool where there was a rocky ledge. The others followed, looking concerned. David had run down to the edge of the water and helped haul Mohammed out.
"Are you ok, Mo?" he asked.
"Yer, thanks to Olly here. Thanks, Mate."
"It's nothing! What happened?"
"I'm not a strong swimmer and I've only ever swum in a pool back home so I guess I just panicked."

Once everyone was back up with the group, Florence sought out Oliver.

"You bloody idiot!" she shouted at him. "It was pretty obvious he wasn't comfortable about jumping but no, you have to chuck your macho insults at him." Oliver just looked at the ground and didn't make eye contact with her until she turned on her heels and walked off.

"Oh, what a hero!" chimed Simon and Nancy, a little later.
"Not now, Guys. I'm not in the mood," pleaded Oliver.

Day 15
Florence was initially left alone with her book but she was soon joined by Simon, who had bonded well with the women in the group. "Hello gorgeous," he said, flicking his scarf over his shoulder. "Can I join you?"

Most men were wary of Florence when they first met her, sensing the steel barriers she surrounded herself with but Simon was openly gay and clearly very comfortable in his own skin. He was tall and handsome, and much more confident than other men of his own age. He could talk to Florence about art and literature with an ease that she didn't experience with other men of a similar age.

"Yes, of course, Simon, I'd appreciate your company. I've been deserted by Nancy who is setting a web in order to capture Oliver."

"Oh!" said Simon. "Do tell more. I'd like to capture him in my web too!"
"Oh, you're incorrigible!" sniggered, Florence. "You're all welcome to him."
"Well!" said Simon. "I wouldn't be sure he has eyes for Nancy or myself, young lady!"
"Oh stop it now! You've got a very vivid imagination!" she laughed. "Anyway, I thought you had a partner back home."
"Yes, I do but we're having a trial separation which is why I decided to take my mind off things with this trip."
"Oh, I'm sorry to hear that! I hope you work things out."
"Yes, so do I. When we first met there was real sexual chemistry," he said, leaning forward as if sharing a secret. "We used to have sex several times a day," he laughed and made a flamboyant gesture with his hands.
Florence squirmed and felt herself going red at Simon's intimate revelations.
"The trouble is," he continued, "the shine soon wore off and we started to argue about petty things like the colour of the sofa and where to go on holiday."

Day 19

Florence went down to the reception to ask how to get to the local bank. Whilst she was waiting in a queue, she saw Oliver approach. Panicking, she looked for escape routes but there were none and before she knew it he was standing next to her.

'Very avant guarde' he said, commenting on her t-shirt. She was convinced he was ridiculing her and suspected he thought she would not understand him.

Bristling, she went in for the kill. 'Yes, very! But can you name the artist?' She kept her focus firmly on him and enjoyed his discomfort.
'Not so confident now, are you!' she thought, with relish.
'No, but I'm sure you're going to enlighten me,' he replied.
'Piet Mondrian. Dutch pioneer of abstract art who developed from early landscape to geometric abstract.'
'Wow!' he said, clearly taken aback. You know your stuff!
'History of Art,' she gleefully declared. 'Oh, and English Literature. I can tell you a thing or two about the Bloomsbury Set and the Romantic Poets too if you like.'
'Where did you study?'
She sensed his caution and decided to go in for the kill. 'A college in a provincial town.'
'Oh,' he said. She felt she could almost smell the sneer on his breath! She'd save his next humiliation like a coveted bar of chocolate.

Day 20

Akemi showed Florence photos of her wedding. She flicked through the photos of a bride in a traditional white dress; looking beautiful on a sweeping staircase, under cherry blossom, at the beach and in the forest. "You look stunning!" said Florence. "Can I see a photo of you with your husband?" she asked.
"Oh no, I have no husband."
"Oh, I'm sorry," said Florence. "When did you divorce?"
"No divorce. I don't marry. I just have photos."
"Oh", said Florence, "Why?"
"It make me feel good."
Florence felt rather awkward so didn't pursue the reason why someone would want to have wedding photos done without having a proper wedding. She had long been fascinated by the quirky culture of modern day Japan so was not entirely surprised. She was keen to travel to Japan so she asked more questions about Akemi's homeland and looked at photos of her trip to Kyoto where she had taken creative selfies for her instagram with her friends. They were immaculately dressed and had perfect smiles. Florence was able to return the complement with photos of herself and her friends at London landmarks that seemed to captivate Akemi who told Florence she was a big fan of the Queen and Harry Potter.

Later, Florence googled 'wedding photos without a wedding'. The results showed it was popular for women in Japan to have the wedding experience without the groom. She was perplexed and discussed it with Nancy who was equally confused.

Day 22
A few days later, Florence noticed Nancy was regaling Nick, Mohammed and Oliver with a full run down on Akemi's wedding photos and that they were having a good laugh.
"It's certainly a weird place," commented Oliver.
"Don't they eat cats in Japan?"
"No, you idiot, you're thinking of China and they eat dogs!" laughed Nancy.

Florence saw red and marched over to berate them.
"I'm very surprised at you Nancy!" said Florence.

"Oh, for goodness sake!" said Nick when she'd gone. "She's obviously implying the rest of us are the lowest of the low!"
"Yer! No doubt, we're immature idiots." said Oliver. "Why does that woman make me feel like a naughty school boy whose about to get a detention."
"Can we sue her for deformation of character, Nick?" asked Mohammed.
"Well, you heard Olly, 'immature idiots', probably a hard one to prosecute in your case Mate!"
They laughed and noticed Florence glaring at them from the other side of the room.

Day 23

The next day, however, Florence observed Oliver sat in the hotel cafe bar having coffee with Akemi as she sat nursing a green tea and reading her book. She couldn't hear what they were saying but they were clearly animated and she could see that Akemi was laughing and smiling at him. At one point she got Oliver to pose for a selfie. Florence desperately tried to focus on her book but much to her own annoyance she found herself obsessing about what they were talking about. "No doubt he loves the idea of his image being passed around Japan," she thought.

"Come on Florence!" she said to herself in her head. "Just read your book and ignore him. He's not worth bothering about." However, at this point she saw Oliver get up, kiss Akemi on the cheek and start walking toward the exit which was near where she was sitting. She pushed her book up higher in order to ensure he didn't see her. She felt very self-conscious and couldn't get the feeling out of her head that she was a Peeping Tom. When he got near to her he suddenly noticed her. She felt the blood flood to her face and knew she had gone very red.
"What are you reading?" he asked, coldly.
She let the question hang in the air for a few seconds before replying, "Bruce Chatwin".
"Oh, the travel writer," he said with thinly disguised triumph and walked off.

"Urrr!" she heard herself trying to release the tension she felt. "How does he know that?" she thought. "Most millennials wouldn't choose to read Bruce Chatwin but Florence prided herself on not being your average millennial. The idea that Oliver Fraser might not be your average millennial didn't fit with the profile she had drawn up of him; one she was reluctant to redraw any time soon.

Much against her better judgement, she went and joined Akemi. They chatted for a while about their travels so far but before long Florence heard herself saying, "You and Oliver had a long chat."
"Oh, yes!" she said smiling, warmly. She clearly had good memories of this encounter.
"He speak Japanese!"
"I'm sorry?" said Florence, assuming she had misheard or misunderstood. "Did you say, he speaks Japanese?"
"Yes, he live there for a year."
"Oh," said Florence, surprised to hear this.
"He love Japan! We talk about it! He is a very good man. Handsome! Very handsome!" she laughed. "My friends in Japan think he like a film star."
Florence looked horrified. "Have you said this to him?"
"Oh, yes and he laughed!" said Akemi
"Ok, Akemi," said Florence, with a rising sense of frustration, "this is what you need to know about men like Oliver. It's not a good idea to stroke their already inflated ego. Best not to say those things to him in future."

♦

Akemi looked blank. She obviously didn't understand what Florence was saying. She got close to Florence and whispered in her ear, "I think I love him."
"Oh, I give up!" Florence heard herself muttering with much frustration.
Akemi just continued to smile. Much was lost in translation! "He get lots of likes!" she enthused, unknowingly twisting the knife further.

Day 24

After a long day, Oliver and Mohammed were lounging around on their beds before dinner. "Wow!" cried Mohammed, grabbing Oliver's passport from the bedside table. "That's a great mug shot, Olly! You can't look at that without thinking Wormwood Scrubs!"
"Yer, right," said Oliver. "Let's see your passport photo. Bet you look like a jail bird too! It's all that 'don't smile, look straight ahead, no hair over your face, plain white background'."
"All you need is a board in that photo and you're up for murder and facing 30 years!"
"More like 50 if that Florence comes near me again. She's so uptight!"
"Yer, I agree! Mind you, she's hot."
"Oh, for God's sake, Mo, is sex all you think about? Don't worry, she wouldn't look twice at either of us."
"I don't know about that, I think you could be in with a chance, Mate! Mr Universe and all that!"
"Oh, shut up! Anyway, I'd rather suck on a lemon!"

"Are you sure about that? I'd settle for 'Friends with Benefits'."
"Are you kidding?"
"Yer, I know my place!" mused Mo ruefully.

Day 25
Around the camp fire, the group started talking about how they had saved up for the trip.
"I sold my car," said Nancy. "I'll just get an old banger when I get home. It won't look pretty but it will have been worth it. The walk today was stunning."
"I had to work back to back shifts in my dad's restaurant!" moaned Mohammed. "And he's a really hard task master. I just about got enough to pay for the trip but there was no extra left for all those exciting activities like mountain biking, white water rafting and rock climbing."
"How about you, Olly?" asked Mohammed.
Oliver had been keeping quiet, clearly trying to avoid the conversation.
"He's probably got a trust fund," said Florence with a harsh tone to her voice.
"Yes, my parents paid towards the trip," he said, fixing her with a cold, hard stare. "Is it a crime? How did you pay for your trip?" he asked, biting back.
"Oh, I paid my own way," she said, emphasising the word 'own'.
"Did you work as a pole dancer?" joked Mohammed.

"Oh, I'm not staying to listen to this! I'm going to bed!" said Florence, getting up so swiftly that she knocked her stool over.
"That was a bit out of order!" Matt told Mohammed.
"I'm inclined to agree!" said Nancy.
"Oh, she deserved it!" said Oliver. "She's quite happy to dish it out but she doesn't like it when the shoe's on the other foot!"

"I guess, I'm going to have to apologise tomorrow to old Flossy Flow," Mohammed told Oliver later as he climbed in to his sleeping bag. "Mind you, I'm going to savour the image I've got in my mind of her gyrating up and down that pole for now! Night!" he said with a cheeky grin on his face.
"Oh, that's disgusting," laughed Oliver.

Day 27
Young children were selling their meagre wares at the roadside and some of the group got off the coach to buy fruit and drinks from them. Florence had some finger puppets with which she entertained the children. She made them laugh and then gave the delighted children the puppets to play with.
"That was amazing!" said Angela. "No common language but you really connected with them."
"Yes, life's really hard for these kids. They're probably supporting their families and don't go to school."
"Yes, we don't know how lucky we are in the U.K." commented Oliver.

"Well that's ok for you to say," said Florence rounding on him. You're a white upper middle class male. If you were a poor white working class woman then you may not feel so lucky."
"Oh, I don't know, by comparison, women in the western world have a much better deal than those in developing countries where their lives are often controlled and they have little power," he said, clearly bracing himself to fight back. "In the west they've been able to vote for about 100 years and that has led to much more equality, including for working class women. In many dictatorships where the populace can't vote, women are more disadvantaged because the society is very male dominated."
"Two wrongs don't make a right!" said Florence. "Gender bias and the glass ceiling are alive and well in the U.K."
"Oh, get off your soap box!" snapped Oliver, walking off.

Day 29

During a tea break, some of the group got in to a serious conversation about racism and sexism. "I think I have it much easier than my parents," said Mohammed. "Yes, I've had morons call me 'Paki' but most people are much more enlightened these days. My Mum and Dad had to endure it on a daily basis in the past. Some places wouldn't serve them and would tell them to clear off."
"We've had dog muck put through the door by BNP supporters," said Fatima, a social worker from

London. "They targeted all the black families in the area but when we reported it to the police, they just shrugged. Said there was nothing they could do." "That's disgusting!" exclaimed Florence. "You're right! There seems to be less racism today but I suspect much of it has gone underground. People don't say it out loud any more but some still think it. There remains a big problem with racism in Football." "Yes," said Mohammed. "When I go to a game, you still hear monkey noises and openly racist chants. They ban people if they catch them but they don't always catch them."

"Black footballers do have it tough but at least they have powerful clubs behind them. Many powerless black women have a much tougher time. Have you heard about black women who bleach their skin with bleaching cream to lighten it, such is the power of lighter skin? And men of colour can be guilty of perpetuating that myth too."

"That's shocking!" responded Florence. "One of my bugbears is all those statues of white men in cities around the U.K., many of whom got their hands dirty during the colonial period and as slave traders. Do you know that there are more statues of goats than there are of women?" commented Florence.

"What do you think?" asked Florence, looking at Oliver.

"I think that whatever I say will be wrong so I'm keeping quiet."

"Well, typical! Anyone that keeps quiet and doesn't call out racism and sexism is culpable, if you ask me!"

"Well, I think you've just proved my point! But before you inflict anymore of your sanctimonious feminist diatribe on us, can I correct you?" said Oliver with obvious venom.

Florence looked shocked at his response but before she could reply he continued, "There are more statues of goats than non-royal females. Get your facts right!" he said with undisguised triumph.

Florence paused, clearly trying to compose a stinging response. "Oh so that makes it okay, then?"

"Did I say that?" sneered Oliver.

Florence faltered.

"No, I didn't," he said, looking her directly in the eye before leaving.

"Well, I think that was Oliver 1, Florence 0!" said Mohammed sarcastically, enunciating each syllable in order to heighten Florence's discomfort. "You know Oliver's a feminist, don't you?" he continued.

Florence looked incandescent with rage. "If he's a feminist then I'm mini mouse!" she spat back at him.

"Great!" said Mohammed with an air of confidence that unsettled Florence in a way she couldn't explain to herself. "I'll look forward to you eating your words, Mini!"

"Are you a feminist Mo?" asked Fatima.

"I'll pass on that one," he smiled. "I've spent too much time living with my Pakistani dad to have much experience of it," he joked. "But," he said, "turning his attention back to Florence, "with Olly as my mentor, I'm sure I won't be the same sexist man I used to be when I go home!"

"Oh, I can see it now! You'll be a regular Gemaine Greer by the time you land back home!" This time it was Florence's turn to be sarcastic.

"Who?" asked Mohammed.

"I rest my case!" sneered Florence with an air of triumph.

"I'll just ask Olly," he replied, winking at Fatima so Florence couldn't see him.

"I have to say, Florence, I do think you may have misjudged Olly," said Fatima.

"Really!" said Florence with an air of incredulity and a shake of her head.

Day 30

When Florence fumbled around in the dim light for her clothes, she realised that she didn't have any clean t-shirts. She asked Nancy if she could borrow one of hers until she could get to the laundry later in the day. Nancy, who was still not out of bed, had grunted which she took to be affirmative.

It had rained over night and although the skies had cleared, Florence focused on the rocky path which was

slippery, to avoid falling over. The voice came from behind and lassoed her in to freezing on the spot.
"Why are you wearing my t-shirt?"
It was cold but neutral. She was forced to turn round. Oliver was leaning back against a tree and whilst his overall stance was casual, his body language was defensive. He had one leg bent up so his trainer was against the tree and his knee pointed at Florence, and his arms were folded.
"It's Nancy's t-shirt," replied Florence, feeling her face redden and her whole body tense.
"No," he said, slowly, "it's mine. I lent it to Nancy."
"Oh, sorry," said Florence, feeling horrified and as if she was being pulled in to the eye of a storm, a maelstrom from which she couldn't escape. "I'll go and change."
She fled back up the path.
"No need to on my account," he shouted after her but by the time it reached her it was very faint.

When Florence returned, Nancy was only just waking up.
"Why didn't you tell me this was his t-shirt?" asked Florence, tension evident in her voice.
"I'm sorry?" said Nancy, looking bemused.
"This t-shirt," said Florence, starting to sound irritated. "I've just had Oliver Fraser tell me it's his!"
"Oh, the t-shirt! Yes, it is, he lent it to me a few weeks ago when mine got wet in that storm."

Florence started to feel her flesh creep and ripped the t-shirt off. It was at this point that she realised it wasn't an American National Park in somewhere like Arizona or Utah as she'd assumed when she'd borrowed it to go to breakfast but an image of a rock climber hanging precipitously from an overhang on a sheer rock cliff. In small letters it said "Peak District National Park".

Florence threw the t-shirt at Nancy. "Why have you still got it?" asked Florence, aggressively.
"Because I don't want to give it back," said Nancy, burying her face in it. "Um, it smells of him. Just his odour gives me an orgasm!"
"Oh, grow up Nancy! You need to be careful. He's dangerous."
"Oh, don't be ridiculous, Florence. You're the one that needs to grow up. Why would you think he's dangerous?"
"I can just sense it. You need to be careful, Nancy!" Florence pulled on one of her own dirty t-shirts and left without saying another word.
"Well I guess I'm going to have to return my prized possession now! Thanks a lot, pal!" shouted Nancy after her. "And I don't remember inviting you to wear it!"

When Florence got to the breakfast tent, she could see that Oliver was sat with his usual crowd. They were laughing and she imagined how this played out. She also imagined storming over there and confronting him only to find the others looking confused and decided to let sleeping dogs lie. When Nancy came in, she didn't give Florence a second look and went and sat next to Oliver. Florence knew the t-shirt had given her this excuse and she felt herself seethe with anger.

Simon sat with Florence, sensing her isolation. "Hello, cupcake." It was just the soothing interaction Florence needed to take her mind off the earlier incident. She explained what had happened to Simon who took hold of her hand. "You need to let go of all this negative energy, honey, it's not good for your gorgeous complexion."
This made Florence smile. "You're so beautiful when you smile," he reassured her. "Mind you, I get where Nancy's coming from, I think his t-shirt would give me an orgasm too."
"Oh, now you've just spoilt everything!" joked Florence. "One minute it was a therapy session and the next it's a nightmare."
"Oh, you're too harsh on the boy. He's gorgeous. I'm going to hypnotise you one day and you'll wake up and agree with me."
"Some how, I very much doubt that!" smiled Florence. "And anyway, you don't want the competition do you?"
"Sadly," said Simon, mimicking a dramatic Pantomime dame, "I fear the handsome Oliver will never be within my reach." He pretended to swoon and put the back of his hand on his forehead. Florence laughed. "But on a more serious note, Florence, I don't understand what you're scared of."

"No, you wouldn't," replied Florence, cryptically before quickly adding, in order to defect attention, "Let's get a coffee."

Day 31

After four days hiking the group was ready for some down time. Oliver and Mohammed adjourned to a bar in the local town. It was very nondescript but the locals were colourful.

"Well, you did well getting to the top of that pass first, Mate."

"Thanks, Mo. It's all that sport I did at my posh private school."

"Well Florence was dead impressed by you conquering the summit!"

"Yer right, but the whole private school thing is a turn off for her. She's an inverted snob."

"What? You sure?"

"Yes, Mate. She wouldn't look sideways at me and all because my parents sent me to a private school. Well, if she's that shallow it's a non-starter for me."

"Well she must have known lots of private school tossers at Cambridge."

"I'm sorry, did you say Cambridge?"

"Yes."

"As in Cambridge University?"

"Yes. How many of those have you had?"

"Oh, God! What a fool! She told me she went to a college in a provincial town. She knew I'd think college literally and in a back water. She knew I would never assume she went to a Cambridge College. I walked right in to that one."

Florence felt very relaxed, after a hard slog in the mountains for four days, when she joined the others in the bar. She could feel her whole body loosen up and when Obi bought a bottle of wine and offered her a glass she accepted. The group reminisced and laughed at their antics. "I can't believe you sweet talked that guide in to carrying your ruck sack for two days, Ang!'
'I promised him a package of goodies!' she said.
'Woh, the mind boggles! said Matt.
"Yes, I think his did but all he's getting is chocolate and sweets. And don't even think about telling him that I'm a lesbian!"
"You're a lesbian?" said Mohammed, confused. "You kept that quiet!"
"Well, I only tell trusted friends," said Angela.
"Why?" asked Mohammed.
"Oh, really? How do you not know that? Lesbian women are abused verbally and physically all the time by morons who are prejudiced," said Florence.
Mohammed got very flustered and asked, "Are you a lesbian too?"
"Oh for the love of God!" cried Florence but she didn't respond to him.
"No, Florence is definitely not a lesbian, Mo!" laughed Angela.

Florence didn't notice her glass being refilled and continued to sip it, becoming more light headed by the minute. She hadn't drunk alcohol for many years so she had forgotten its effects and was enjoying the light headed feeling that made her feel very relaxed and forget all her troubles.

When they eventually adjourned for the night they had a very steep climb to their hotel. Florence could feel her head swimming as soon as she stood up. She tried to pull herself together and said, "Let's do this" but it was as if she was above herself looking on. She struggled for about 100 meters and Mohammed jokingly started pushing her up the hill until she crumpled and collapsed to the ground. There was still a long way to go up the steep incline and it was becoming clear she wasn't going to make it. Oliver was further up but he paused to glance back. He waited for the others to cajole Florence to continue but when this did not work he descended the hill and picked her up, throwing her over his shoulder, fireman style.

'I'm not sure she's going to like that!' observed Nancy as Florence hung down like a jelly fish.
'I don't think she's got much choice!' laughed Mohammed. 'But I wouldn't want to be in his shoes in the morning when she's sobered up.'

At the hotel, he unceremoniously dumped her on her bed, put the bin next to her and crouched down to talk to her.

'This is in case you want to be sick. Oh, and I know you went to Cambridge, that bastion of privilege. Rather hypocritical after you've lectured me.'

"I got there on merit!" she snarled at him before she pushed him away, so hard that he fell back on to the carpet.

'A simple thank you would have sufficed,' he said and left.

Day 32

The next morning, Nancy plonked a large glass of water on Florence's bedside table. "Waky, waky!" Florence groaned. "Did that jerk really carry me up the hill yesterday?"

"Yes, he did," said Nancy but I think you'd still be there if he hadn't so I wouldn't complain too much. Come on, we leave in 45 minutes but we need to have breakfast first. Don't worry, I'm sure he'll steer well clear of you but I might add that he came back later to check how you were and jerks don't tend to do that, do they Florence?"

Late in the afternoon, the group sat in the hotel garden after a long day. It was warm, the flowerbeds were colourful and birds were singing to create a very positive ambiance.

"Being here makes you feel miles away from the trials and tribulations of home," said Nick. "I earn a good wage as a solicitor but I still can't afford to buy even a one bed flat in central London and my rent is crippling.

I've managed to start saving for a deposit but it is still going to be a few years before I can afford a flat and it will be a bit further out and in a less fashionable area."
"I know the feeling," said Fatima. "Since my divorce, I've only been able to afford to rent but rents have risen exponentially in the last decade."
"Oh, you're just depressing me now!" chipped in Mohammed. "I think I'll still be living with my parents when I'm middle aged! I can't wait to escape and I think they'd like to get rid of me too but there just seems to be no end in sight."
"Well, sooner or later, the economy will improve because it goes in a cycle so I'm sure you'll escape at some point!" said Oliver.
"Well that's easy for you to say. Most of us don't have the beauty of the bank of Mum and Dad to fall back on," responded Florence.
Suddenly, and without warning, Oliver got up from his chair which went flying backwards and shouted angrily, getting very close to Florence's face, "Don't assume you know anything about me!"
Florence cowered back in her seat and Nick grabbed Oliver by the arm and pulled him away.
"Hey, Olly! Calm down!" he said. Oliver shook him off and strode off, kicking the chair out of the way. At the same time, Florence burst in to tears and ran off in the other direction, sobbing.
The other members of the group were left looking awkwardly at each other. "Whoa, what happened there?" asked Mohammed.

"I'm not sure, Mo. It seemed to kick off without warning. I don't think those two are enjoying this trip. It's a lot of money wasted if you don't have a good time."
"I think they've both brought some baggage with them," said Fatima. "They should probably avoid each other's company in future. They're not good together. You two speak to Olly and I'll have a word with Florence. They're both lovely on their own but when you get them together, sparks seem to fly."
"Well she's the aggressor, if you ask me!" responded Mohammed. "She always picks on Olly. He was just acting in self defence."
"Yes, I have to agree with Mo!" said Nick.
"Well that may be the case but let's just try and keep them apart from now on."
"Fine by me!" said Mohammed. "I'm in Olly's camp so tell her to stay away from me too!"

Later, Oliver went to Florence's room with Nancy who confirmed that she was there. They found her curled up on the bed with her back to the door. He didn't go into the room but stayed at the threshold. "Look, I'm very sorry I shouted at you like that. It was wrong of me but I stand by what I said. You don't know anything about me or my past or my life today. I'll stay out of your way in future." Florence didn't respond and Oliver retreated.

Late in the day, Nick and Mohammed dragged Oliver out for a drink at a bar, well away from the hotel. He was reluctant to leave the hotel room but they refused to take no for an answer. "We promise you we won't bump in to her," said Mohammed. "We're going to act as your body guards from now on to protect you from her!" He put on his dark glasses and pretended to talk in to a microphone in his sleeve. Oliver laughed and allowed them to lead him to a bar on the other side of town.

"I bet she's in to bondage!" said Mohammed. "She probably likes tying some poor guy up and torturing him during sex."
"Oh, you've got a vivid imagination, Mo!" said Nick. "I don't know where you get your ideas from. I think she's more likely to be frigid. She seems to hate men and I don't think she has any kind of sex with them."
"Oh, can we stop talking about her!" moaned Oliver. "Let's change the subject. If the worse comes to the worse, at the end of this trip, we'll never have to see her again. She can go off and pick on some other poor guy."

Day 33

After breakfast the bus drove across a flat valley lined with straight rows of vines as if standing to attention. The ubiquitous mountains rose up in the distance like a protective barrier for the amber nectar that the group was going to taste. They drew up at a large, attractive, modern building with plate glass windows that gave picture perfect views of the vines. They started with a tour of the vineyard and the production processes before they went to the spacious tasting room. Here their guide gave them tasting notes for the selection of white, red, rose and sparking wine on offer to taste.

Initially, most took it seriously, recording preferences and trying to spot the 'hint of raspberries and citrus" but as time went on and the wine started to dull the senses, most gave up on the serious side of the wine tasting. It was at this point that Mohammed noticed that Florence was not swallowing the wine she tasted but was discarding it in a bowl and swigging water in between tastes. "Oh, I see you like to spit rather than swallow!" he joked with Florence.

"Oh, for God sake!" said Florence, sounding angry.

"I'm not putting up with this." With that she promptly got up and moved to the other side of the tasting room, well away from Mohammed.

"Is it something I said?" joked Mohammed.

"You know exactly what you said, Mo!" laughed Nick.

"Yer, but she didn't have to react like that!" said Oliver. "She's such a drama queen!"

"It's her right to react how ever she likes" chided Angela who had been quietly observing the exchange.

"She's probably got some gorgeous middle aged man at home so she has no time for the immature comments of you sex starved young bucks!"

"Oh, don't mince your words, Ang!" said Nick and anyway Mo is the sex starved immature one making the inappropriate comments so I don't know why you're picking on me and Olly!"

"Her middle aged guy is welcome to her!" mused Oliver.

Later that night Mo and Oliver were in their room lounging on their beds and listening to music. "Let's play 'marry, shag, kill'," said Mohammed.
"Play what?" asked Oliver.
"Have you never played 'marry, shag, kill'?" asked Mohammed. "Oh, you haven't lived! I'll go first so you get the picture. OK, so I'd marry, um, Laura, good child bearing hips! I would definitely shag Florence; she'd be so impressed she'd want more and probably become my sex slave, and I'd kill that woman at the bar who embarrassed me by asking for ID! Your turn!"
"Um!" said Oliver, sounding uncertain. "I'd marry the lovely Nancy, shag Jemma with the long legs and kill Florence! Not a bad game this!" he concluded.

Day 34

Oliver did his best to keep his distance from Florence throughout the day which was spent at a local town and historical museum. At the end of the day, however, dinner was on long trestle tables and they ended up closer for comfort than they would have liked but still maintained their silence. When the meal ended, Mohammed asked Oliver if he wanted to get a drink in the bar.
"Yer, mate, that sounds good," replied Oliver.
"Ok, brother, let's go!"
Oliver's reaction took everyone by surprise. He looked horrified and said quietly, "Please don't call me

brother." He got up and instead of heading for the bar he went towards the room.

"Oh!" said Florence, gleefully. "He doesn't like us lower classes calling him brother. Says it all!"

"Oh shut up, Florence!" said Mohammed and with that, he got up and left.

Those left looked uncomfortable, including Florence who buried herself in her book to avoid further discussion on the matter.

Mohammed returned to the room where he found Oliver with his head in his hands. He'd been crying.

"I'm really sorry," Mohammed said. "You're a good mate and I don't want to upset you."

"No, Mo, it's me who should apologise. I thought I could come here and put it all behind me. Just be myself. But I can't."

"I don't get it. Of course you can be yourself. You are yourself"

"That's the problem. I don't want to be just myself."

"You're losing me, Olly"

"Yer, I know. It's complicated."

"Well, try me!"

A long pause ensured in which they both sat in silence, looking at the floor, Oliver started talking and it all spilled out. "I'm one of identical twins. My twin was killed in a car crash when we were 16 years old. Even though it was seve years ago that I lost my other half, my mirror image, it seems like yesterday. We were telepathic, lived parallel lives, and then one day his life was snuffed out just like that by a drunk driver who mounted the curb. I lost my soul mate. We would have done this trip together."

"Oh, God" said Mohammed, not quite sure what to say. "I'm so sorry, Olly." He put his arm round Oliver and they just sat together in silence for a long time.

Day 35

The next morning Mohammed found Florence before breakfast, making sure she was alone.

"I'm sorry I was rude to you yesterday Florence but you've got Olly all wrong and you need to give him a break. Do you understand?"

"No," said Florence. "Enlighten me."

"I can't. It's not my place but you'll regret it if you carry on the way you have been. Take it from me," he said, his voice started to break.

"Oh," said Florence, looking both confused and contrite.

Mohammed abruptly turned on his heels and walked off.

The programme for the day was to explore the local town 'at your leisure' which for many meant sitting in the town square with a drink. On a long tour which involves only up to 3 nights in any one place, it is a luxury to be able to slow down and get off the treadmill of constant travel for a while; a chance to recharge one's batteries.

Florence, Angela and Fatima had coffee together. The square was a hive of activity and everyday life. Groups of women sold souvenirs to tourists and elderly women in black headed for church.

Fatima, a black woman in her early forties, was older than the average group member but fitted in well. She had gained the confidence of Angela and Florence and they chatted openly and freely to her.
'So what brought you on this trip?" asked Florence. "I mean, don't you have a job and kids and stuff like that?"
"Work have let me have a sabbatical," replied Fatima after a long pause. "I had a messy divorce last year and my mental health suffered. No kids.....sadly."
"Oh!" said Florence, feeling as if this was the second time she'd put her foot in it in 24 hours.
"So," said, Fatima, clearly trying to change the subject, "when did you come out, Ang?"
Florence squirmed, feeling that Fatima was being rather direct but it didn't seem to bother Angela in the least. "Well, it's complicated really," she replied. "First I had to come out to myself. You know, admit to myself that I'm gay. In Northern Ireland most people are extremely conservative and religion is very prominent. At the age of about fourteen I kept telling myself to fancy the boys like the other girls did but I just couldn't get my head round that. I felt disgusted with myself for being attracted to girls and there was just no one to talk to about it. My dad still won't speak

to me. Oh, he does talk to me but only about the basics and he is very cold. I told my Mum first and she's been supportive but I don't think she actually understands."

"Have you got a girl friend?" asked Fatima.

"No, not at the moment. I've had a few but they haven't lasted for long."

"There's plenty of time!" reassured Fatima. "Look at Florence here. She scares every man who even looks sideways at her. Even with those looks it will take years to find a partner," joked Fatima.

"What do you mean?" asked Florence, looking genuinely shocked. "I've got high standards!" she said, relaxing.

"Yes, so high that no one meets them!" They all laughed out loud and called the waiter over to refill their coffee cups.

At this point, Florence noticed that Mohammed and Nick were a few tables away but Oliver was not with them. This was very unusual.

Morning melted in to afternoon and Florence, Angela and Fatima decided to visit the local museum. "We'll just be here all day ladies if we don't move now!" said Fatima, "Come on, shake your booty!"

They spent several hours at the museum and realised that Fatima was impressively knowledgeable about ancient civilisations. "The practice of sacrifice was

very brutal but they did genuinely believe that they were doing it to please their gods."
"Oh, that's an excuse is it?" laughed Florence.

They returned to a bar in the square as the sunset and were joined there by Nick. "Where are Mo and Olly?" asked Angela.
"Olly's not well and Mo's gone back to check on him."
"What's wrong with him?" asked Fatima. "Not serious, I hope."
"Yes, it is I'm afraid but it's not my place to give details. Can I get anyone a drink?" he asked, trying to sound more upbeat. When he went off to get the drinks the others looked at each other uneasily.

Mohammed arrived back at the hotel and found Oliver curled up on the bed staring at the ceiling. "I've come back to check on you Mate. I'm worried about you." Oliver sat up and Mohammed noticed he'd been crying again.
"I really appreciate that, Mo."
"Do you want to tell me about it?"
"It was just past our 16th Birthday and we were walking back from a friend's house. Henry was right beside me when the drunk driver mounted the curb and just ploughed in to him. I instinctively jumped clear and....." his voice started to break up.
"Take your time Mate. I'm not going anywhere"
"I remember his head thudding onto the pavement and bouncing like a melon. The car drove off and I

remember screaming and shaking Henry. Some of it is a fog but I think I was dragged off him and the next thing I remember were blue flashing lights. I was in a police car following an ambulance and my parents and sister were waiting at the hospital." He broke down again and Mohammed put his arm around his shoulder.

"His death was confirmed at the hospital but I knew he was dead from the second his head hit the pavement."

"I don't know what to say, Olly. I'm so sorry," said Mohammed with tears in his eyes.

"You don't need to say anything, Mo. Just having someone listen to me helps. Life was just a blur for many months. I stopped eating and lost loads of weight. My A Levels really suffered but the teachers were great, and my friends at school. They gave me space. I was supposed to become a boarder with Henry but I couldn't face it so I just stayed as a day student. I had counselling with my family and on my own for years and I still do but although the pain has dulled a bit, it's still just below the surface. I know it will never go away. And I feel so guilty."

"Why do you feel guilty?" asked Mohammed.

"I didn't know to start with but a psychologist I saw said it's not uncommon. Even gave it a name. Survivor's Guilt. I went to a group called Twinless Twins. That really helped because I met other people like me. Some had lost their twin to suicide and some to cancer and so on but only they knew how I really felt. Don't get me wrong, my poor Mum, Dad and sister were in agony but it was just different."

"We'd always talked about travelling together so it's very hard to be doing it on my own. Sometimes I feel as if he's here with me but most of the time I feel as if he's disappeared in to a black hole. It's hard. Florence is right about my family being rich but we'd all give that up in a blink of an eye if we could have Henry back."
"Oh, just ignore Florence. She's got issues of her own. Everyone thinks she's a snotty cow."
"What do you mean by issues?"
"Oh, I don't know. I can't put my finger on it. But I don't think she's a happy person."

They fell silent and looked at the floor.

After what felt like a long period of time, Oliver said, "Do fancy a drink in the square, Mo. It would be good to lighten the mood!"
"Sounds like a plan!" said Mohammed.
"Mind you, I can't cope with running in to Florence at the moment. I can't face any of her barbed comments"
"Don't worry mate, I'll see her off for you."
"No you won't!" laughed Oliver. "You're scared of her."
"Yer, you're right, petrified. She's in the bar with the girls so we'll slip out the back!"

Day 40

On the bus, Mohammed and Oliver discussed the day's events. "I wish I was doing rock climbing with you!" moaned Mohammed. "My budget wouldn't stretch to any extras so I've got to do the boring guided walk."

"Yer! I wish you were doing it too! When we get home I'll take you to the Lake District. My parents have got a place there and we can go rock climbing. I can show you all my favourite spots."
"Wow! That sounds great Mate. I'll hold you to that!"

Once at their specified location, David announced where the group would need to meet according to their chosen activities. "If you're doing rock climbing you need to get back on the bus," he said. The mountain bikers need to go over to the hut over there and Sarah will take rest on a guided walk."

Once on the bus, David checked the list of rock climbers. "Where's Mo?" he asked Oliver.
"He's not doing rock climbing."
"Well he's on my list." He opened the bus window and shouted, "Oi, Mo! Come and get on the bus."
"I'm not down for it! Can't afford it!" replied Mohammed.
"Well someone's paid it for you. Come on, hurry up, you're holding us up!"
Mohammed did as he was told and got on the bus.
"Was this you?" he asked Oliver.
"No, definitely not me!" he replied. "Can you imagine the stick I'd get from Fossy Flo if I paid? *'Oh, he just*

thinks we're all peasants and he's giving us patronage!'" he mocked, doing a very credible imitation of Florence.

When they got to the site, Mohammed and Oliver were split in to beginners and advanced. "Good luck, Mate! I'll look forward to hearing all about it!" said Oliver.
 "I guarantee you'll be hooked like me."

When the group met back at the bus, Mohammed was clearly elated by his rock climbing experience. "It was amazing! Don't get me wrong, it was scary when you look down but I loved it. Are we still up for the trip to the Peak District, Olly."
"You bet!" said Oliver. You'll be advanced by then if your secret benefactor keeps funding you."
"My what?"
"Secret benefactor, someone who funds you secretly. Or perhaps it's a stalker. Someone who's obsessed with you."
"Hey, Dave!" said Mohammed. "Who paid for me?".
"I couldn't possibly say!" said David. "It's more than my life is worth."
"Are you sure it wasn't Olly?"
"Yes, I can confirm that. You're barking up the wrong tree there. Look in a more unexpected direction and that's all I'm saying or I'd have to kill you!" he joked and walked off to meet the other members of the group.
"Unexpected, eh," said Oliver. Perhaps it's Florence and she has a secret crush on you."

"You think?" said Mohammed. "Perhaps she's trying to get me fit so she can rip all my clothes off and have red hot sex with me!"
"I'd like to see that!" said Oliver.
"Oh!" said Mohammed. "That's a bit purvy"
"I don't mean literally, you idiot! And we both know it's never going to happen!"

"How was your rock climbing?" asked Nancy?
"Challenging," replied Oliver. "The advanced section was very steep without many obvious foot holds."
"I'm sure you coped, with muscles like that!" laughed Nancy.
"Do you fancy yourself as James Bond?" asked Florence, sarcastically.
"Yes!" said Oliver, looking her in the eye, "so long as you're not my Bond Girl!" he snapped before he turned and walked off.
"Wow!" said Mohammed. "You're dicing with death, standing up to her like that!"
"Well someone has to."

"Do you fancy a coffee?" said Fatima who had observed the earlier exchange with Oliver.
"Yes, that would be good," said Florence.
They walked out in to warm sunshine and found a quiet back street cafe where they sat in a secluded alcove. Fatima bought them both coffee and cake.
"I hope you don't mind me saying," Fatima said cautiously to Florence, "but you are always very hard on Olly. I'm no expert but my job involves reading

people's personalities on a daily basis, and my feeling is his heart is in the right place."

"I'm sorry, Fatima but you can just tell from the way he speaks that he is arrogant and entitled."

"Ok," said Fatima, "so you don't like the way he speaks, presumably because he has an upper middle class accent but what is it that he has actually said and done that you don't like?"

Florence looked uncomfortable. "Well you've heard him. He has no concept about the lives of poor women back home."

"I disagree," responded Fatima. "He was, quite rightly, pointing out that women in the west are in a better position than many in poorer countries. I've had first-hand experience of this. As you know, I'm from Sierra Leone and women certainly don't have many rights there compared to the U.K. Not many young men of his age would have any idea that women in different parts of the world are not equal."

Florence looked at the floor and didn't make eye contact.

"You're clearly very passionate about defending the rights of the weak and vulnerable, Florence but I hope I'm not going to offend you when I say I worry that your interaction with men suggests that you have trust issues." There was a long pause. "Oh, listen to me!" continued Fatima. "I'm supposed to be on a break and I'm sounding like a counsellor. Just ignore me!"

"You're right," said Florence, quietly.

"Do you want to talk about it?" asked Fatima.

"I'm not sure I can."

"Well you know where I am if you need to talk," said Fatima. "And I can give you details of organisations that can help when you get home. I need to go to the bank. Shall I meet you back at the hotel?"
"Yes," said Florence.
"And remember, you know where I am."

With that, Florence was left with her thoughts. Painful thoughts that she had tried hard to suppress. She started to hyperventilate and knew she needed to get out of that confined space and get some air. She quickly found a park and sat on a bench, trying to focus on the colourful pallet of flowers on display in the beds around her but she couldn't stop him getting in to her head. The man who raped her. The man who came back to her room, held her down and raped her. She put her head in her hands and sobbed.

"Florence," whispered Fatima, putting her arm round her shoulder. "I saw you from the bank and followed you. I hope you don't mind."

Florence couldn't speak but she put her head on Fatima's shoulder and continued to sob. It was a long time before she took a deep breath and started to tell Fatima her story. The story of how she'd been date raped at university. How she didn't give consent and screamed out but no one came. How a friend went with her to the police and how he was arrested. How the police said there was not enough evidence and how she had to face him on a regular basis in lectures and around campus before she left university, scarred and angry.

"I don't know what to say Florence," said Fatima, her voice shaking with emotion.

"You don't need to say anything," she said. "You listened and you're sympathetic."

"Have you had professional help?"

"No, my friends were very good and rallied around but it was near the end of our time at university and we soon went our own ways. I couldn't tell my Mum, it would break her heart."

"What about your dad?"

"He had an affair and left my Mum when I was very young. He didn't stay in touch. My Mum is very protective of me because it's always just been the two of us."

"You can't suffer alone, Florence. You need to talk about this with people you trust and people trained to help. There are lots of support groups where you'll realise you're not alone."

"So are you saying I should talk to my Mum?"

"Only you can decide that but ask yourself if she would be happy knowing you are suffering like this?"

"You were spot on about my trust issues with men. I worry that I will never have a healthy relationship and all that comes with that."

"I'm guessing you're feeling a great sense of loss."

"Yes!" said Florence. "On that day I lost my carefree, happy go lucky personality. I got on well with the boys at school and had boyfriends but I don't let men anywhere near me now."

"Yes, that's understandable but it's not a way forward. Do you feel as if all men are potential rapists?"

"No, but I can't work out which ones are and which aren't; after all, I let a rapist in to my room and I feel guilty about that."

"Do you think you are letting the rapist win?"

"I knew you were going to say that, and I have turned that over and over in my mind but I just can't work out how I can stop him winning. I guess I'm weak."

"I haven't known you for long Florence but the one thing I do know about you is that you aren't weak. You're a strong young woman who has been damaged but you will repair yourself over time and with help. I promise you. Please trust me. I've worked with women who have been sexually abused and raped, and I'm not saying it will be easy but I have seen women turn their lives around. You just need to have faith. I noticed how captivated you were with those children by the roadside. Do you want to have your own children?

"Oh, yes! I desperately want children and I know that could be hard. I've even thought about using a sperm bank in the future."

"Do you want your children to be without a father like you?"

"No."

"Well, we'll have to work on that then won't we," laughed Fatima, trying to lighten the mood. "Now I

think you owe me a drink," she said, "I got the coffee and cake."
They linked arms and returned to the hubbub of the old town.

Day 47

Florence and Fatima became very close and were seen together deep in conversation on a regular basis whether it be over a meal at the hotel, on the bus or when hiking. Florence confided that she had struggled with anorexia after the rape, which had been of great concern to her Mum. "I became obsessed about what I ate and would weigh everything. My Mum insisted I go to the doctor and they did refer me for counselling. She identified that I was suffering from low self-esteem and I should have told her about the rape but I couldn't bring myself to talk about it."
"You have to Florence. I really advise you to get professional counselling when you get home. You've got lots to work through and you can't be expected to do that on your own."
"I know," said Florence, hugging Fatima.

"Do you think they're lesbians?" Mohammed asked Nick.
"Haven't got a clue. Ask Ang, she knows about that sort of thing."
"Hey, Ang, come over here. Are Fatima and Florence lesbians?"
"Oh, get straight to the point Mo, I should. You're a bloody idiot, you know. And no they're not lesbians.

"Well they spend a lot of time together."
"So! They're women and women talk to each other about their problems."
"What problems?"
"Oh, like I'm going to tell you. Piss off!" Angela walked off and left Mohammed looking furiously at Nick.
"Great idea, mate!"
"I was only joking when I said ask Ang. My guess, for what it's worth, is that Florence has got problems and Fatima is a good listener."

Day 50

"Do you mind if I set you a challenge, Florence?" asked Fatima.
"It depends what it is," responded Florence, laughing.
"Make friends with, Olly."
"Oh, I wasn't expecting that as a challenge," responded Florence.
"I've been so unpleasant to him, he will probably just want to stay well clear."
"Well, I had Mo speak to me the other night. He said he'd heard I was a good listener and he wanted advice on how to help, Olly."
"Help him with what?"
"Well, I don't feel I can break his confidence but I will say that the two of you have more in common than you think. I know you think he's privileged and feels entitled but from what Mo told me, that couldn't be further from the truth. Oh, he does come from a rich

back ground but his life has been far from privileged. Just try and get to know him and it may be a comfort to both of you."

"I'm not sure what you're getting at but I'll do it for you, Fatima."

"No, you won't, you'll do it for yourself."

Day 53

It was an early start and Oliver was first on the bus. He dozed off and woke up to find Mohammed taking pictures of him.

"Pack that in," he shouted at Mohammed, slapping him round the head and grabbing the phone to delete the photos of himself, mouth open and looking like a guppy fish.

"Ow, that hurt!" screeched Mohammed.

"Good!" said Oliver. "It was meant to! And if you don't stop it, I'll tell Flossy Flo what you say about her behind her back!"

"Oh, go on!" laughed Mo. "Do you think she'll punish me? I have a vision in my head of her in a dominatrix outfit with a whip in her hand!"

"Oh, hi Florence!" said Oliver convincingly over Mohammed's shoulder. "You ok?"

"You're kidding me!" mouthed Mohammed.

"Yes!" said Oliver, "But it got you worried! Pay-back time!"

Day 54

The next day was another early start for the beginning of a 4-day hike. The group met in the foyer for a briefing. David talked them though the route and they discussed the challenges they would face.

"Now that we are in a dry and arid region," explained David, "it is very important that you remain hydrated. You all need to carry water and there will be extra water carried by the support vehicle."

"Now, I'm aware of the injuries and medical conditions that the group has but now is the time to make me aware of any new conditions."

Oliver looked at his feet and was aware of eyes boring in to him.

"So has anyone got any questions?"

"Have you got the cold beers in the ice box?" laughed Nick.

"No alcohol until tonight I'm afraid, Nick. But I'm sure you'll make up for it at the campsite!"

"Too right!" replied Nick.

There was a two-hour drive to the start of the trail. It was still dark and cold when they set out but an orange glow soon appeared on the horizon as a spectacular backdrop to the silhouetted black mountains. Eventually the large, bright orb started to edge up over the mountain, casting long shadows over the landscape.

By the time they got to their location, it had started to warm up. Oliver picked up his packed lunch from the box and put it in his ruck sack but he got distracted by

David who needed his help to unload the cage on top of the vehicle. As he returned to his back pack he caught Florence picking it up and slinging it over her shoulder. "Hey!" he said. "That's my ruck sack."
"So!" said Florence, turning on him. Are you saying a girl can't carry your ruck sack?"
No!" said Oliver, putting his palms up defensively. "I wouldn't dare!"
"Good!" responded Florence. With that she turned on her heels and marched off.

"Did you see that?" said Oliver to Mohammed and Nick.
"Yer!" said Nick. "Weird if you ask me!"
"Mind you, I heard her side swipe about sexism. She can't help herself. Watch yourself, Mate. Those rattle snakes have got nothing on her," joked Mohammed.

Florence stayed at the front of the group but, unusually, Oliver remained near the back of the pack. They wound their way through a narrow gorge with the cries of eagles overhead and then crossed a steep rocky hillside to the pass before descending on the other side.

After three hours of hiking Oliver cautiously approached Florence to retrieve his rucksack.
"Thanks! I haven't felt too great so it really helped to have 'a girl' carry my ruck sack!" he said, smiling at her.
"Well aren't you going to sit down?" she asked.

He was so astonished, he paused.
"If you don't want to, it's not a problem," she responded in a very neutral tone, passing him his bag.
"Oh no," he said, "I'd love to."
He sat down on the other side of the rock she was sat on.
"Stunning scenery!" said Oliver, trying to disguise his nerves. "It brought back my A Level Geography."
"Yes," replied Florence. "It's very other worldly. I feel as if I'm on the moon."
"I keep expecting R2-D2 to come round the corner!"
They both laughed and visibly relaxed. The small talk continued until the end of lunch when Oliver returned to walk with the boys and Nancy took the arm of Florence.

"I did try to persuade Nick to come and rescue you," said Mohammed, "but he's chicken."
"Like you then Mo," laughed Oliver. "Well you'll see she didn't eat me alive and I'm still in one piece!"
"Ohhhh!! She can eat me alive anytime!" said Mohammed.
"You've got a one track mind, Mo! Come on you guys! Let's set the pace!"

After a challenging morning, Florence was happy to fall back with Nancy.
"So!" said Nancy, "Are you two an item now?"
"Oh, don't be ridiculous, Nance. Just because I carried his bag and had lunch with him doesn't mean I'm about to rip his clothes off and jump in to bed with him at the

earliest opportunity. It was an olive branch, or should I say Oliver branch, and nothing else!"
"Good, because I still live in hope!"
"You're welcome to him; I still think he's a stuck up git!"

Day 57

After the highs and lows of the four-day hike, the group gathered in the main square for a drink. Nancy was pulling Mohammed's leg about his fear of spiders and Angela was playfully threatening to tell his dad about his beer drinking. When the waiter approached they hardly noticed him and carried on talking. He stood patiently and then shouted something loudly to his fellow waiter by the door. Suddenly, much to the surprise of everyone, Oliver flew at him and grabbed him by his t-shirt. He shouted aggressively at him before releasing him and pushing him away.
"What the hell?" exclaimed Nick.
Everyone looked shocked as Oliver took some deep breaths.
"What happened there?" asked Fatima, looking concerned.
"He was making lewd comments about the women in the group," replied Oliver.
"And what did you say to him?"
"Shut the hell up or I'll cut off your testicles and shove them in your mouth," said Mohammed as if he had been the one who had said it.

"Yer, right," laughed Oliver. "I just told him to get lost."

"Since when did you speak the language?" asked Florence.

"Since my Mum worked here in the embassy. Come on guys, let's go somewhere else. We don't want them spitting in our drinks!!"

Day 58

The next day, Florence was engrossed in the game of a small child playing in the dirt beside the bus. He was clearly doing sound effects as he pushed a car through the loose gravel. The bounce of the seat as someone sat next to her brought her back in to the bus and she turned her head to be greeted by Oliver. "Alright?" he said without expression and much to her surprise, her stomach turned over and she felt what she could only describe as an electric shock convulse through her body.

"Fine, thanks." she replied, and before she could say more, she became aware that he had gently placed his hand over hers as it lay on the seat beside her. Was this an accident or deliberate? She found herself uncharacteristically flustered and her heart was pounding. It was a fleeting moment because Mohammed called to Oliver from the front of the bus to come and help load the cage on the roof of the bus. By the time he re-boarded the bus, Akemi had sat next to Florence but there was no going back now, Florence couldn't get him off her mind. Had she misjudged him? Was she letting him, against her better nature, steal her heart? Why did he seem to have a magnetic pull on her?

Day 59

"My parents had an arranged marriage," said Mohammed. My grandparents arranged it back in Pakistan and the next thing my dad knew was he was back there getting married to my mum. They hardly knew each other. Hard to believe really."
"Well good job they did arrange it for him," said Florence, "or we wouldn't have you!"
"Ah, that's sweet!" smiled Mohammed.
"Any chance they can arrange a marriage between us?" said Mohammed, playfully.
"Would you want an arranged marriage?" asked Florence, looking curious.
"Absolutely not but I think my Mum has other ideas. 'You should marry a nice girl from my village'!" he said, mocking his mother's accent. "Little does she know that I lost my virginity when I was 14 with Melanie Smith, behind the P.E. container on the school field."
"What the hell is a P.E, container?" asked Oliver.
"Oh, for god sake, Mate. You don't have them at posh private schools. It's literally a disused lorry container that you put balls and javelins in because they've sold off most of the school to build a new housing estate.

Anyway, what you should be asking is, 'did she have big boobs and a nice bum?'."

"O.K. Mo, did she have big boobs and a nice bum?"

"Oh, yes!" he said, miming the 'big boobs', "trouble was, I later found out she'd had sex with at least half the boys in my year group! It kind of took the shine off it."

"What sort of a school did you go to?" asked Chloe.

"A rough one!" said Mohammed. "It was always in trouble with Ofsted and teachers came and went like a Number 10 bus. In class, I didn't get a look in. I just kept my head down and taught myself most of the time."

"You, not get a look-in!" exclaimed Oliver. "I can't imagine that."

"Well it's true! There were lots of gobby gits who just wanted to wind up the teachers. It wasn't so bad at A Level as they weren't in those classes. They were bumming around in retake and Level 2 Voc classes."

"But you went to a good uni so it couldn't have been that bad." commented Oliver.

"Oh, I'm sure it was," said Florence. It sounds like my school."

"Your school?" asked Oliver, looking at her as if she was on a different planet.

"Yes, Olly. It was a world away from the school you went to. Mo must be intelligent to have survived that. He just hides it well!!" she said, laughing loudly.

"I'm not sure whether to take that as a compliment or not!" said Mohammed.

"Take it as a compliment, Mo," laughed Oliver. "It's all you're going to get out of Her Ladyship. Get it in writing too!"

Florence swiped Oliver playfully around the head before he grabbed both her arms, pinned her down and attempted to tickle her. She laughed uncontrollably!

The rest of the group looked uncomfortably at each other, unused to the changing relationship between Oliver and Florence. Later that evening, when they were alone in their room Mohammed questioned Oliver about it. "So how come you and Flossy seem to be flirting with each other all of a sudden?"

"Oh, I wouldn't call it that! replied Oliver, looking embarrassed. "But she certainly seems to be trying to make an effort to be nice to me. I'm not holding my breath because I'm sure it won't last!"

Day 60

When the group reached the ancient ruins in the mountains they gasped at the spectacle of the stone buildings and dry stone walls, suspended amid steep vegetation rich mountains. The guide explained that there was much mystery about the function and purpose of the site, which had long been abandoned but it was rumoured that children were regularly scarified by this sophisticated civilisation.

"It really turns my stomach!" said Nancy when they sat down for a break at the end of the guided tour. "How could they sacrifice children? It's just evil."

"You have to be very careful not to project our twenty first century sensitivities on to the past," replied Oliver. These people were very reliant on satisfying their gods to please them. Normally they would sacrifice what was valuable to them. In years of bad harvest there would be mass starvation so they genuinely thought they were doing the right thing to offer children for sacrifice."
"I still can't get my head round it!" said Nancy.

"What's the worse thing you've ever done?" Mohammed asked Nancy.
"Oh, that's a hard one!" she joked.
"It was probably when I was about ten years old and I kidnapped the neighbour's dog."
"You kidnapped a dog!" exclaimed Florence!
"Yep! I was desperate for a dog but my parents wouldn't let me have one so I just kidnapped one. It was simple. I lured it with a few doggy treats and took it to the bottom of our garden. Now when I say garden, we lived right out in the countryside so we had a wood at the end of the garden. There was a shed there so I popped the dog in and returned on a regular basis to feed it with tip bits from the house. I'd even walk it down in the woods. About a week after I'd kidnapped it, posters appeared all over local neighbourhood. At this point, I was forced to 'find' the dog. I even got a reward for finding it and local radio rang up and interviewed me about what a heroine I was!"
"Did you feel guilty?" asked Florence.

"Oh no, I revelled in the attention. I was only ten, remember. I don't think I've ever confessed before!" she laughed. "We live in a very small community so if I mentioned it to anyone it would be all round town within an hour, even now. Luckily the neighbours moved away a few years later and took the evidence with them but I've never told my parents!"
"Well a quick call to your local radio station should sort that!" joked Oliver.
"Come then Olly, I've bared all so it's your turn."

"Well," said Oliver, "I did get caught but it took about six months. My mum and dad went out to a party when I was about fourteen and my brother and I polished off a bottle of my Mum's very expensive gin. We just filled it with water and popped it back in the cupboard. I guess we knew we'd be caught at some point but you live for the moment at fourteen so we just forgot about it. We got caught big time when my Mum's boss and his wife came for dinner. She gave them gin and tonic when they arrived and they must have been far too polite to mention it was not right. They sipped away at it until my Mum had one and realised it was all tonic and no gin! Once they'd left she went mental. My dad found it funny and I think he got in to more trouble than we did." He paused and seemed to go in to a world of his own. Mohammed sensed that he was replaying fond memories of times with his brother in his head.

"Well I can top the both of you!" said Mohammed.

"Why does that not surprise me, Mo?" laughed Florence.

"Well, when I was fifteen I borrowed my dad's car," he said, miming speech marks when he said the word 'borrowed'. "Mum and dad had gone up the road so they walked and weren't expected back until the early hours so I borrowed the car to get me to a party only 2 miles away. Luckily, it was automatic so easy to drive. Trouble was they got back much earlier than expected and my sister snitched. The first I was aware of being in big trouble was my dad storming in to the party and shouting my name. He practically had steam coming out of his ears! Mind you, good job he didn't come ten minutes earlier because I was upstairs snogging Angela Brown. I'd only popped down to the kitchen to get a beer which I did manage to shed before he grabbed me by the scruff of the neck and dragged me out. As you can imagine, it was very embarrassing and I never lived it down at school, but the worst of it was the bollocking I got at home. You'd think I'd committed mass murder! What if I'd been caught by the police, run over a child, totalled the car......it just went on and on. He threatened to take me down to the police station the next day and have me banged up. That was pretty scary but looking back I don't think he really meant it. It would have bought even more shame on the family. The worse bit was my mum crying and telling me how disappointed she was in me. I was, of course, grounded for ever and they made me wash up at the restaurant for six months without pay."

"Well your dad does have a point," said Nick. "Getting a criminal record at the age of fifteen is never a good idea!"
"Oh, so have you never done anything illegal then, Nicky Boy?" asked Mohammed.
"Nothing I'm going to admit to," said Nick, "I'd be struck off. I have to keep my nose clean I'm afraid so if I throttle you for being a right git Mo then it's the end of my career!" he joked.

"How about you, Miss Goody Two Shoes?" asked Oliver, looking at Florence.
"Well..." she said, struggling to think of anything. "Nothing that compares to the misdemeanours and crimes of you lot but if you push me I once paid Lucy Bird to write an essay for me."
"Oh, so that's how you got in to Cambridge then?" he laughed.
"Very funny!" she replied, sarcastically. "How did you get in to Southampton University? Oh, don't answer that one, expensive private school!"
"Oh, touché," he said, smiling at her.

Day 61

David announced in the morning that there would be a disco for their group at the hotel in the evening. They hadn't had much time to let their hair down beyond relaxing in a bar so the excitement was palpable and it was the topic of conversation all day.

At the end of dinner, Simon made an announcement, "Ok, ladies, I'm not make-up artist to the stars for nothing. My single supplement room, now, for a pamper session."
There was lots of laughing and squealing as he led a group of girls off like the Pied Piper!

Most of the men were gathered in the bar nursing a pint. "What does he mean by single supplement?" asked Mohammed.
"It means he's paid extra not to have to share with you and your snoring," laughed Oliver.
"Or your smelly socks!" hit back Mohammed. "Does he really do the makeup of the stars?"
"Yes, I think he does," said Nick, "but it's more like C listers such as those on 'I'm a Celebrity Get me out of Here' rather than super models."
Angela joined them. "Surprisingly, I don't fancy a pamper session! My mum tried to get me in to dresses and did my hair in plaits and ringlets for years but it just wasn't my thing."
"Do you think I could take your place?" asked Mohammed.
"Why would you want to take part in a pamper session?" asked Oliver, clearly confused.
"Because he wants to perv at the girls in frilly knickers and bras, obviously!" laughed Nick.
"Well I'm sure you'll defend me in court if I get arrested!" laughed Mohammed.
"I'm afraid I specialise in property disputes not perverts!" said Nick, "So I'd forget that!"

Soon the D.J. was in full swing and the dance floor packed. Oliver couldn't help but notice how beautiful Florence looked in a dress that emphasised her curves and with her long hair cascading down her shoulders. He had never really noticed her before but he was suddenly transfixed, in spite of her terse and antagonistic behaviour, particularly towards him. He had got the impression she disliked him from day one but he couldn't put his finger on why. Until recently, it had not bothered him, she was nothing to him but all of a sudden, she seemed to come in to focus.

Nancy and Florence joined the men but soon most were up dancing, leaving only them with Oliver and Mohammed. Suddenly, and without warning, Mohammed pulled Nancy on to the dance floor and Oliver and Florence were left alone. Oliver felt awkward and he wasn't sure what to say to her, but it was Florence that broke the ice. "I think they've orchestrated this!" said Florence.
"Have they?" said Oliver, looking surprised.
Oliver had his arm across the back of the sofa and Florence moved back so it was as if he had his arm around her. Oliver couldn't believe what was happening but he took a deep breath. "It would be a shame to disappoint them," he said playfully and moved his arm so it was truly round her. She turned her head towards him and they kissed, a long passionate kiss that took them to a totally different place.

"Would you like to dance?" he asked her, and he took her hand and led her on to the dance floor.

Day 64

A few nights later, the group was camping in an attractive valley. They'd become skilled at setting up the tents and preparing dinner so they had more time to relax. It had been a spectacular sunset but after dark the wind started to get up and then driving rain drove everyone off to bed. Sleep was impossible as the wind swirled around the tents and the rain hammered on them. At about 3 am in the morning, Nancy and Florence became aware of shouting and screaming outside.
"What the hell is going on?" asked Nancy with panic in her voice.
"I don't know," said Florence. "What do you think we should do?"
Before Nancy could answer, David put his head in the tent and told them to grab their things as quickly as possible and meet him outside in two minutes. They both felt tense and a rising sense of panic as they rapidly pushed everything in to their back packs.

They stumbled out of the tent and were instructed by David to follow Malcolm, one of their drivers, up on to a ledge 20 meters up the rocky cliff behind the campsite. They immediately did as they were told without question. Other members of the group were already gathered up there and talking about the campsite flooding. It had been a narrow escape.

Oliver noticed Florence shivering so he enveloped her in his coat until she was cocooned and then he pulled her in close. She tingled all over and her pulse rate reached a crescendo as she gave in entirely to him. He moved closer and kissed her on the lips, caressing her hair gently. She felt as if there was an orchestra exploding in her head and she let herself savour the moment.

The busses were moved to higher ground where the group had to spend the rest of the night. Oliver refused to take his coat back and Florence snuggled next to him on the bus but she did notice that he looked cold and pale, in spite of his refusal to let her give him his coat back. She gradually stated to feel drowsy and was surprised that she could enjoy being so close to a man after so long. Soon she entered a deep sleep.

Day 65
 As the sun's rays infiltrated the bus, Florence woke from her deep sleep with a start. Her subconscious had not caught up with the events of the night before and she expected to wake in her tent. Much to her horror she was presented with the vague profile of a man and visions of her attacker flooded her head. She gasped and started to hyperventilate.

Taken by surprise, Oliver, who had woken earlier and enjoyed the sensation of Florence asleep in his arms,

moved away, aware that his presence was making her panic. "What's the matter?" he asked. Are you ok? Do you need some water?" He saw Florence start to calm down as he spoke to her and gently took her hand. "Is that ok?" he asked. She nodded.
"I'm sorry!" she replied. "I had a bad dream."
"You looked at me as if I was a monster!" he joked.
"You are, I mean, you were in the dream!"
"Oh, ok," he said, looking confused.
By now Florence had relaxed and put her head on his shoulder. "Now I'm awake I can see that you're definitely not a monster!" she said, trying to sound light hearted.

The tents were strewn all over the hillside and it took a while for the group to gather them up and load them on the bus because they were still heavy with the deluge of the night before. Fortunately, the next night was at a hotel so the tents could be dried and everyone could recover from the ordeal and a broken night's sleep.

"Do you fancy going for a drink?" Oliver asked Florence after dinner.
"Are you asking me out on a date?"
"Um, yes, I guess so!" he laughed. "Please don't turn me down because Nick and Mo are watching and I think they've got money on you saying no!" he joked.
"Well let's make sure they lose their money then!" she smiled, linking arms with him. "Where to Mr Fraser?"

"Anywhere you like. You pick and the drinks are on me. Well if that's ok with you. I don't want to be accused of being sexist!"

"No, I'm fine with you paying," smiled Florence. "So long as you let me pay next time."

"Oh, I'm pleased to hear there's going to be a next time!"

"Well that does depend on how tonight goes!" she joked. They found a quiet alcove in a cosy bar and became so engrossed in each other that they didn't notice time pass, that the bar had emptied and that the staff were dropping heavy hints that they wanted to close up.

Day 66

"You're certainly rising to my challenge!" joked Fatima.

"I know!" said Florence. "I keep having to pinch myself. I'm ashamed to say that he's not at all like the guy I imagined he was."

"You don't say!" mocked Fatima. "I hate to say I told you so, but I did!"

"Yes, you did! And so did Nancy and everyone else."

"He sounds so much like my attacker that I just projected him on to Olly. Now I've got to know him, I don't even think about that anymore. I feel so bad about the way I've behaved towards him."

"Listen, Florence. You have got to get beyond the guilt. The way you feel is only natural. You were badly let down by an evil man. Take your time but

talk to him and tell him that is what you want to do. He's a kind and sensitive man. Hopefully, if this develops, you will be able to tell him about the rape but only when you're ready."
"Yes, thanks Fatima. I know they all think I'm stuck up and up tight but I just can't help but put a ring of steel around myself for protection."
"That's perfectly natural," Fatima reassured her.

"Hello, You," said Oliver, coming over when he saw Florence.
"Hello, You too!" smiled, Florence.
"I'll leave you both to it!" said Fatima.
"Oh, I'm really sorry, Fatima!" said Olly. "I didn't mean to ignore you."
"Oh, don't worry, Olly! I know you only have eyes for Florence," she joked. "I'll see you two love birds later."

"I think they're all having a good laugh at our expense", said Florence. "I guess we are the most unlikely couple."
Oliver sat down next to Florence and they chatted easily to each other alongside checking social media and sending messages home.
"Oh, bloody hell!" said Florence, getting frustrated with a message she was trying to send. Why does predictive text bring up James and John every time when I'm trying to message Julie?"
"Algorithms were invented by men. They've very sexist!" said Oliver. "It's the same with the

technological world in general. Men are safer in cars because the crash dummies used to improve safety are based on male bodies."

"Is that so?" asked Florence, lowering her sunglasses. She couldn't hide the fact that she was impressed.

Day 67

The bus wound its way up the steep mountain road towards the pass, exhibiting a throaty roar and plumes of smoke as it struggled against the steep gradient. Some people dozed and some took photos of the spectacular views. Mohammed was in the process of making his latest vlog post, but was getting frustrated by the unwanted contributions of Nick and Oliver who were making fun of him.

As the bus came round a sharp hairpin bend it suddenly encountered a landslide. Malcolm, the driver, had to swerve sharply and then try to correct himself but the bus was out of control and it went bouncing down in to a deep ditch, tipping on its side. Everyone gasped and screamed, and some were crying as the bus eventually came to a rest.

"Is everyone, ok?" shouted David with rising panic clear in his voice. There was no response so he tried moving down the bus to check which was difficult because of the 45-degree angle. In addition, it became evident that the exit was blocked. David and Malcolm kicked open the sky light to open an emergency exit. "Ok!" announced David, "We're going to have to climb

out of the emergency exit which isn't going to be easy. We need to move as quickly as possible so we can get you to safety. Leave all belongings in the bus. David climbed out of the sky light to help people once out of the bus and Malcolm and Oliver helped others climb up on to the seat arm and then the head rest to access the emergency exit. When Florence got to the head of the queue, Oliver noticed that she had a head injury. "Your head's bleeding, Florence!" he said, sounding concerned.
"Is is?" asked Florence, instinctively touching her head and looking at the blood on her hand. "I hit my head on the roof when we crashed but I'm fine."
"No, you're not," said Oliver, firmly. I'm following you out and I'm going to get first aid for you. Nick, can you take my place when I get out," he said, focusing on getting Florence through the emergency exit. Once outside he found a large boulder for her to sit on.

Nancy came over to see how she was. "Oh, don't you start!" said Florence. "It's worse than it looks."
"Sit down next to her Nancy and don't let her move!" ordered Oliver. "She's not being a very good patient!" he said, sounding frustrated and walked off to get the first aid kit that the bus carried.
"Oh, he's so masterful!" joked Nancy.
"Oh, stop it Nance. You're a disgrace to the sisterhood."
"I don't care" announced Nancy. "He can administer first aid to me any day of the week!"

Oliver returned with antiseptic, cotton wool and a large bandage. "Right!" he said, "Sit still."
"Yes, Doctor Fraser," laughed Florence but when he cleaned the wound it stung and she winced.
"Are you ok?" he asked, looking concerned.
"Yes!" she said. "Get on with it."
Once the wound had been cleaned Oliver bound the bandage round her head and checked it was secured tightly.
He then took both her hands. "Are you sure you're ok?"
"Yes!" she said, "but thanks for looking after me. What would I do without you?"
"You don't have to do without me!" he said. "I'm not going anywhere and I'm going to make sure you get lots of rest."
David and Fatima came over to check her and reinforced what Oliver had been telling her about resting. "Did you black out at any stage?" asked David.
"No," replied Florence.
"Well that's good. You won't be concussed but we will get you checked over by a doctor when we get to the town where we are staying."

David and Malcolm flagged down a passing truck which helped them pull the bus out of the ditch using a tow rope. The entire group cheered to see the bus back upright. They checked it outside and in before they would allow the group to return to it.

"You're sitting next to me, Young Lady!" said Oliver. "I need to keep an eye on you!" Nancy gave her a 'you lucky devil' look but she didn't argue with him.

Once back on the bus and sat with Oliver, Florence was overwhelmed with a great sense of emotion. She welled up and large tears dripped down her cheeks. Oliver put his arm round her and wiped away her tears. "You're suffering from shock!" he said. "It's understandable that you feel upset."
"I really want my Mum!" she said.
"I know," he said. "I want mine too." Oliver hadn't been involved in a road accident since the death of Henry and he was aware that the trauma of the two were starting to become intertwined. "You'll have to put up with me," he joked, trying to lighten the mood.
"You're just fine!" smiled Florence. "A great second best!"
"Oy, you!" he said, tickling her.
"No, don't do that. You're making my head hurt."
"Oh sorry!" he said, looking apologetic.

Once they were at the town, David took Florence to the doctor's. Oliver wanted to go with them but Florence insisted he should stay and have a coffee with Mohammed and Nick. "I'll be back soon!"

Mohammed was aware that the crash may have brought back bad memories for Oliver. "How are you doing, Mate?"

"Oh, ok but..." he trailed off.
"Yes, I know!" said Mohammed. "Come on, let's get you something stronger."

Florence returned an hour later with a large box of pain killers. "How often do you have to take those?" asked Oliver.
"Twice a day before food," replied Florence.
"Right! I'll be making sure you take them." he said, sternly.
"Right Old Mother Hen, isn't he?" mocked Mohammed.
"Very true!" said Florence, raising her eyes.
"That's a nasty gash on your head. You'll do as you're told Ms Bloom!" insisted Oliver.

Day 68

At the end of a museum tour, the girls went off to the ladies' toilets. When they emerged, Oliver was missing.
"Where's Oliver?" asked Florence, casually.
"He's gone for a drink with the beautiful Antonia, the museum guide," said Nick, not realising he was about to get his friend in to a lot of trouble.
"Why?" asked Florence, clearly annoyed.
"He just wanted to see her artefacts!" joked Mohammed.
"Oh, I give up!" said Florence, irritated by their immature and laddish behaviour.

Florence found Nancy and Chloe and returned to the hotel with them but she couldn't relax. She noticed that Oliver hadn't returned to the hotel when they were all in the bar and that he hadn't returned to the hotel when they went for dinner. Florence left dinner early, feeling tense and restless and she decided to go to her room and get an early night. When Nancy came in several hours later, she still hadn't got to sleep but she was determined to forget him and not give her obsession with him any oxygen. She was not going to ask Nancy when he had returned or, it suddenly struck her, if he had returned.

Day 69

The next morning, it was a "day at leisure" which essentially meant "do what you like". On such days, some would lie in and sit around the hotel whilst others would go out to explore. Florence and Nancy went to breakfast early with the intention of going to the local market to get some souvenirs as presents for the folks back home.
"I can't get too much," said Florence as I'm moving on the Australia and New Zealand after this."
"Are you?" asked Nancy, surprised. "You never mentioned that before."
"I guess it just never came up," said Florence. "I'm on a gap year so I thought I'd get the tough, adventurous bit out of the way and then go on to somewhere that is

a bit more like home. I've got a visa that allows me to work so I may do some fruit picking in Queensland and work in a vineyard in South Australia."
"Sounds great," said Nancy. "I've just got my boring job to go back to. Back to reality. Mind you, the second I get back I'm going I'm going to start saving for my next trip."
"That's the spirit!" smiled, Florence.
"Have you told Oliver about your plans?"
"No!" replied Florence, sounding defensive. "Why would I tell him?"
"I thought you two were loves young dream these days."
"Oh stop it, Nancy. And anyway, he went off with the Museum Guide yesterday so he clearly doesn't care for me."
"Ohhh, sounds as if you're jealous!" laughed Nancy.
"Absolutely, not!" said Florence, emphatically. "Now are we going to shop for souvenirs or not?"

Oliver, Mohammed and Nick got up late. Breakfast had already finished so they went out to a local cafe and got breakfast rolls and coffee. They sat at tables on the pavement and watched the world go by.
"Look at her! The curves on that!" said Mohammed, mesmerised by a young woman in a skin tight dress walking past.
"I wouldn't say that anywhere near Florence," said Oliver. "You'll get a lecture on objectifying women."

"Oh, don't worry," said Mohammed, "She's too busy being angry with you Lover Boy to focus her feminist anger on me."
"Me?" questioned Oliver, looking genuinely shocked. "What have I done?"
"Oh, you are naive!" joked Nick. "Have you ever had a girlfriend before?"
"No," said Oliver.
"What a good looking guy like you?" asked Mohammed.
"Well, life has kind of passed me by since we lost Henry," said Oliver, starting to well up.
Mohammed and Nick shared a 'we need to tread carefully here' look.

"Have you ever been on a date, Olly?" asked Nick.
"No," replied Oliver. "Well unless you count the time I went with a girl to the British Museum to see an exhibition and we got lunch at the cafe in the atrium."
"No, we don't count that!" exclaimed Mohammed. "Well not unless you had a quickie in the disabled toilets."
"You haven't had a quickie in the disabled toilets at the British Museum, have you?" asked Oliver naively.
"No, of course not. I've never been to the British Museum but I could give you the low down of my conquests in pubs and clubs around town."
"Oh, shut up Mo. We're here to help Olly, not discuss your seedy sex life."
"It's not seedy," said Mohammed, looking offended. "I'm known locally as a stud."

"Good job you're not a woman," said Oliver. "Or you'd be slated for that kind of behaviour!"

"So, are you a virgin then?" asked Mohammed.
"Oh for goodness sake, Mo!" said Nick. "Pack it in!"
Oliver just looked down at the pavement.
"Let Uncle Nick and Uncle Mohammed take you in hand!" laughed Nick, lightening the mood.
"Sounds like a recipe for disaster to me!" smiled Oliver. "What did I do wrong?"
"Yesterday, after the museum tour, you went off with the beautiful Antonia."
"Only because she's got a PhD in ritual sacrifice."
"I'm sorry? A what, in what?" asked Mohammed.
"Ritual sacrifice!" said Oliver, starting to sound irritated.
"Well she certainly sacrificed you to Florence. She was furious you disappeared."
My dissertation at university was on ritual sacrifice and it's an area that I'm interested in. We got chatting and she asked me for coffee. She's a bloody mother of two young children."
"Well it probably didn't help that Mo here told Florence you'd gone off to look at her artefacts."
"Oh, cheers, Mo!" said Oliver, looking angry.
"Well she did have big knockers, you have to admit that one." Nick gave him a hard stare as if to say, 'stop right there.'
"Look, Mate, Florence didn't know you went off to discuss her dissertation or that she's a young mother with kids. As far as she's concerned, you've gone off

with an attractive woman. You're just going to have to grovel a bit, get her flowers or something. Ask Simon too, he'll know what will make her tick. You really lack experience with women!" laughed Nick. "Mind you, in the long run, it's a good sign. She's clearly jealous as hell so you've got her in your spell!"
"What spell?" asked Oliver.
"Oh, I can see we've got our work cut out here, Mo! It's going to be a long term project!"

The boys found Simon later. "Get her a pretty necklace or bracelet!" he advised. "What's her favourite colour, Olly?"
"Haven't a clue!" said Oliver, looking totally out of his depth.
"Green," said Mo, "and she likes abstract art or the impressionists."
Oliver looked astonished. "How do you know all this, Mo?"
"I worked that out in the first couple days, Mate," laughed Mohammed. "If you've got all day, I could go through everything else I know about our Ms Florence Bloom, a really hot chick."
"Oh, just ignore him, Olly. He picks out the girls he fancies and then finds out what he can so he's got loads of cheap chat up lines. They never work."
"Some do!" said Mohammed, looking offended.
"What on Florence?" asked Oliver.
"No! Obviously not!" said Nick, firmly. "He's been chatting girls up since he was fourteen so he's got years of experience."

"I've got a really good one that worked well on, Katie Anderson," said Mo.
"Stop it, will you," said Nick. "We're trying to help Olly out here and I can't see any of your chat up lines working on Florence.

"Give me an hour. I'll get something sorted." said Simon and true to his word, he was back within an hour with a bouquet of flowers and a beautifully wrapped package.
"Oh, that looks amazing! I am sure it will do the trick. Thanks, Simon." said Oliver.
Nick and Mohammed raised their eyebrows to the sky and tutted. "One thing you need to know is that when you apologise and give these to her she going to tell you to get lost!" said Nick. "But she won't mean it."
"Oh, I'm totally out of my depth now!" groaned Oliver.
"You just need to trust us!" Mohammed laughed.
"Yer, that's what I'm worried about!"
At that moment he spotted Florence sit down on the other side of the bar to read her book. She hadn't seen them.
"Go on!" said, Nick. "Get it over with!"

Oliver took a deep breath and walked over to her, forgetting to take the flowers and gifts. He approached her from behind and put his arms round her. "Hello, gorgeous!"

Florence jumped out of her skin and shouted at him. "What the hell did you do that for?" she snarled. "You nearly gave me a heart attack!"

This was the sort of reception Nick and Mohammed warned him about so he wasn't put off.

"Look, I'm really sorry I went off yesterday without saying anything. It was unforgivable."

"What makes you think I'm worried?" said Florence. "You can do what like with the dear delightful Antonia!"

"It's just that I got talking to her and her PhD was similar to my dissertation at university. She only had a shot time to discuss it because she had to pick her kids up so we went for coffee round the corner. Then I went to get something I'd seen at the market for my mum, in case the seller wasn't there the next day."

He could see her body language change in an instant and he sensed he had turned a corner and may have the advantage but he persisted with the grovelling that Nick had suggested. "I know, I'm really selfish and I should have left you a message to say where I'd gone. Am I forgiven?"

"Oh, stop the puppy dog eyes and come here!" laughed Florence, hugging him. Out of the corner of his eye, he noticed Nick, Mohammed and Simon. They'd been watching everything, and were frantically gesturing to the flowers and present.

"Wait there!" he told her and dashed over to pick them up.

"I'm getting the hang of this! Thanks, Guys!" he said, grabbing the flowers and present.

"Don't worry, you owe us a pint later if you don't want us to tell her we gave you all your best lines."
Oliver smiled and went back over to Florence to continue the charm offensive.

"Oh, so you and Olly have kissed and made up then," observed Nancy, later.
"Yes! I'm rather ashamed to say that it was all a misunderstanding and I got the wrong end of the stick, but I'm not telling him that. Look at the bracelet he bought me. It's exactly what I would have bought myself!" she laughed.
"Yes!" said Nancy, knowingly, having chatted to Simon about it earlier.

"Well done you for making it up with him!" said Fatima. "So often, relationships break down because couples don't communicate. Listen to me! I'm sounding like a counsellor again!"

Day 73

The bus roared in to action and moved off. It was a long and steep climb in to the mountains and the bus drove back and forth on a series of switch backs with terrifying drops in to a deep and steep sided valley covered in thick vegetation. At several points there were small shrines and crosses to mark spots where people had plunged to their deaths and a reminder of the danger they faced. Once at the car park for the waterfall walk it was a short walk and they could already hear the roar of the falls about a kilometre down the track. On the journey, Florence looked round for Oliver who she had not seen at breakfast. They were starting to spend more and more time together and she wanted to walk to the waterfall with him. It became clear to her, however, that he was not on the bus. As soon as they got off, she found Mohammed to enquire as to why he was not on the bus.

Mohammed looked worried and this concerned her. "It's not a good day for him so he's stayed at the hotel."
"Is he unwell?" she asked with a rising level of concern.
"No," said Mohammed. "He's not unwell."
"So what's the matter then?" asked Florence.
"He wanted to tell you but he just can't bring himself to talk about it. He said it was ok for me to tell you and I guess this is as good a time as any."
Mohammed proceeded to tell Florence about the tragic death of Henry, Oliver's identical twin brother. Today was the anniversary of his death so a day that was torture for Oliver.
Florence listened intently to everything Mohammed told her. "Oh God!" she said, "I had no idea!"
"No, why would you?"
"He needs lots of support."
"You've obviously been a good friend to him, Mo."
"It's not a problem," he said. "He's a great guy. Hold him close, Florence."
"Oh, I intend to Mo," she said, hugging him.

Back at the hotel Florence asked Mohammed for his key so she could go alone to the room. She found Oliver in the dark, curled up on the bed in a foetal position, clutching a scarf. She took his hand. "I'm so sorry, Olly," she said. They just lay together so close that they could feel each other's heart beats and rhythmic breathing.

After about an hour Florence put the bedside light on and sat up. "Have you had anything to eat or drink today?"
"No," said Oliver.
She got him a glass of water and made him sit up to drink it. "You need to eat, Olly. Most people will have left the dining room and will be in the bar. We can slip in and then come straight back here."
They sat in a quiet corner and Florence went to the buffet for both of them. "I wish you could have met Henry," he said, quietly.
"I can't imagine someone who is identical to you," she said.
"We were so identical that we got exactly the same gcse results but by the time the results were published, he was dead. All that work for nothing."
"How did you do?"
"Really well! Mainly A and A*. It's what got me in to a decent uni because my A Levels were C grades. My teachers pleaded my case on compassionate grounds.

I sometimes dream about him but he's always sixteen. He's never moved on with me. He's never become twenty three so it feels as if he's slipping away from me. I still find it hard to cope with life without him."

She took both his hands across the table and they shed tears together.

Day 74

"Ooooh!" said Simon to Florence. "There's a lot of tension in those shoulders."
"I know," replied, "Florence, "I think I'm getting travel weary. It takes it out of you moving from place to place every few days."
"I've got the perfect remedy!" he chimed, "An Indian Head massage, works every time. And I'll work on those knots in your shoulder. You'll have to come to my room because I've got my massage oil there. Come on!"
"How can a girl resist!" laughed Florence and she allowed him to take her by the hand and lead her to his room.
She sat on a chair, took her hair band out and shook her long hair loose. As Simon started to massage her head she felt her whole body relax and closed her eyes.
"Now let's work on those knots in your shoulder." said Simon, tying her hair back up. She didn't hear Oliver come to the door and swap places with Simon. She continued to soak up the glorious feeling of relaxation

as his hands massaged her and relaxed her tense muscles. She drowsily opened her eyes to see Oliver in the mirror opposite."
"I can stop," said Oliver, immediately.
"No!" she said, smiling at him and placing her hands on his to keep them on her shoulders. "I want you to carry on! Please!"
He kissed her gently on the neck and whispered, "Would you be more comfortable on the bed?"
She allowed him to lead her to the bed where she lay on her front and he straddled her. He dripped more oil down her back. He started with her shoulders and gently worked his way down her spine. She tingled all over and felt a tremendous sense of elation. He turned her over and they held each other tightly so they felt as if they were one. They kissed and cuddled and snuggled together.
"Thanks for not pressurising me, Olly," said Florence.
"Why would you thank me?" asked Oliver. "I would never pressurise you to do anything. But we'd better get back to our own rooms or Mo's dirty mind will be running riot!"
"I need to tell you something, Olly."
"Oh, that sounds serious!" he joked.
"It is," she said, looking at him in anguish. "I was raped at university."
"Oh, my God Florence," he said, taking hold of both her hands. "Who did that to you?"
"Someone I called a friend, a fellow student, a man who I invited back to my room, someone whom I trusted and he raped me." She told him the whole

story and he listened intently. "For a long time I found it hard to be touched by anyone, even my Mum, and I had suicidal thoughts. I feel really ashamed to say this, but I did."

"I don't know what to say," he said.

"You don't need to say anything. Just hold me tight." They both sobbed in each other's arms. "I want to help and protect you," said Oliver.

"I know you do."

"I'm here for you and I'm not going anywhere."

She kissed him one more time before they went their separate ways; Florence reflecting on gentle, thoughtful, kind Olly who had been reborn in her mind.

Day 75

The next morning at breakfast, Florence spotted Oliver and made a bee line for him. She sat on his lap and put her arms round his shoulders. "Missed you," she said, kissing him.

"Missed you too," said Oliver

"Whooooh. It's too early for all that slushy stuff!" exclaimed Mohammed. "Pack it in, the pair of you."

"I've got a bone to pick with you!" said Florence, spotting Simon at the end of the table.

"Sorry, Flo! I couldn't resist his masculine charms," laughed Simon playfully.

"Me neither!" said Florence, kissing him again.

"Oh, I've had enough of this!" said Mohammed.

"Come on Nick! Let's go for that jog before we have to

give the pair of them a cold shower!" The whole group laughed, clearly happy for the new couple.

Day 76
"Today is devoted to working at the orphanage supported by the Travel Company for the last ten years," said David at the morning briefing. "The staff and kids are always happy to see us and we try to use your skills to make it more relevant and worthwhile."

Now on my list I've got Florence and Nancy teaching.

"Oh, let's hope they're doing sex education!" whispered Mohammed. "I'll be signing up for that!"
"Stop it!" hissed, Oliver. "You just can't help yourself, can you?"
 "Nick, there's some legal contracts they'd like you to draw up and I believe Fatima is doing staff training on counselling skills. Matt is down to do some medical checks and some of you guys have signed up for sport with the kids."

It was a short drive to the orphanage where they were welcomed by screaming, excited children.

Oliver, Mohammed and other group members grabbed some footballs and started to have a kick around with the children. "I'll show you how it's done, Olly!" said Mohammed dribbling the ball across the dusty pitch.

"Thanks, Mate!" said Oliver displaying some impressive ball skills that got more attention from the children.
"Messi!" shouted one child pointing at Oliver.
"Ronaldinho!" exclaimed another.
"I thought you said you don't play football!" said Mohammed, looking rather put out.
"No, I said I don't support a team. Subtle difference!" he replied.

As they got back on the coach Florence and Nancy enthused about their day teaching. "Nancy's a natural!" said, Florence. "They loved the activities she did with that blow up globe."
"Yer, and they all wanted to know if Florence knew the Queen when she showed them where she came from!"
"I'd never really thought about teaching in the past but I may have a rethink now," mused Florence.
"Speak to my parents first!" said Matt. "They're both teachers and they've been warning me off for years."
"Yer, I just have to think about a typical day at my comp to put me off teaching!" laughed Mohammed.
 "It was like Beirut most of the time and the teachers were definitely on the front-line. I think most of them had to pop pills to get through the day and one even had a hip flask!"
"Oh, don't exaggerate!" said Oliver, winking at Mohammed, "Britain's got the best education system in the world!"

"Oh, so says the voice of experience!" said Florence, looking very irritated.

"Don't rise to it Florence!" said Mohammed, "He's trying to wind you up."

"And doing a good job!" laughed Oliver.

Florence folded her arms and continued to look annoyed.

Day 77

Florence and Oliver had fallen well behind the rest of the group as they chatted about their childhoods, university and the trip. Suddenly and unexpectedly, Oliver grabbed her hand and started to run towards a small gap in the high rock cliff of the arid desert landscape.

"Where are we going?" asked Florence, sounding surprised.

"Not far," said Oliver, "trust me." As they reached the gap he swept her up in to his arms and carried her across the threshold.

Beyond the gap it opened up in to a stunning gorge with high orange walls of rock that were painted with swirling patterns that could have matched any impressionist painting. They gasped as it took their breath away.

"It's beautiful!" said Florence, wide eyed with admiration. "But what about the rest of the group? They'll get back to the bus way before us and wonder where we are."

Oliver put a finger to her lips. "Stop talking. Live in the moment!"
She obeyed him as he kissed her and caressed her gently. "If you feel uncomfortable just tell me to stop."
"No, I don't want you to stop! For the first time in my life, I don't want you to stop!"
Very much in the moment, she felt drunk with ecstasy as they made love in their rocky cathedral.

Oliver carried Florence's back pack back to the bus so they could make up some time. Everyone else had boarded bus and David was at the door to the bus and looking concerned. "What happened to you two?" he asked, I was getting worried."
"Oh, we're really sorry," said Florence. "I twisted my ankle again so I had to rest a while and Olly had to carry my bag."
"Well so long as you're both ok," said David. "Thanks for looking after her, Olly."
"Oh, it was my pleasure," said Olly, squeezing Florence's hand. They both found it hard to keep a straight face.
"I never knew you were such a good liar!" Oliver whispered to Florence, as they walked down the bus, "I'm going to have to watch you in future," he laughed.

Florence sat next to Nancy and she told her about her ankle. "Why have you got so much sand all over

you?" she asked, eyeing Florence suspiciously, "It's even in your hair!"
"I was in so much pain, I had to lie down," said Florence.

Oliver sat next to Mohammed, further up the bus. "What have you been up to Lover Boy?" he said playfully.
"None of your business!" said Oliver, smiling.
"Any chance of a threesome next time?" asked Mohammed.
"Absolutely not!" smiled Oliver. "And don't let Florence hear you saying that! Your life won't be worth living."
"So, it's true then! The least you can do is give me all the steamy details!" pleaded Mohammed.
"Not a chance, Mate! Find your own sex life you Saddo!"

That night Florence stayed around the fire with the men after most of the women had gone to bed. She enjoyed the warm glow of the fire which compensated for a chilly night. They had finished off the mulled wine that the group had enjoyed and Oliver roasted the last marshmallow and fed it to Florence, making her laugh when she nearly choked on it.

When she decided to go to bed, Oliver said he'd walk her back to her tent. "Oh, there's no need," she told him. "You stay and enjoy her rest of your beer."

"Yes there is," he said, "I'll just worry about you and won't be able to relax."
Florence found this strange. She's never had a man worry about her and want to protect her. She'd just experienced abandonment and violence. Oliver was kind and giving, not like the man who had just wanted to take and give nothing in return.
"I'll be back in ten minutes," said Oliver. "Don't drink my beer!"
"And if you're not back in ten minutes, we know what you're up to in the moonlight!" said Mohammed.
"Oh, shut up, Mo!" said Oliver, smiling.

Oliver put his arm round Florence and they walked up the hillside, through a sea of tents. At one point he tripped on a tent peg and she had to grab his arm to stop him falling flat on his face.
"Thanks!" he said, kissing her. "Sweet dreams!"
"Oh I will!" she said, smiling as she imagined Oliver in her dreams.
"I'd better get back or Mo's over active imagination will be running wild."
Florence crawled back in to her tent and was aware that he waited for a few minutes before heading back down the hillside.

Day 78

Florence was sat with Oliver, Mohammed and Nick for a picnic lunch. It had been a long and hard hike in the morning and they were enjoying time to relax.

"I never buy new clothes," said Florence. "I only buy second hand clothes that would otherwise go to landfill."
"And what about clothes you want to throw out?" asked Oliver.
"They have to be falling apart but then I cut them up and use them as cleaning rags," explained Florence.
"Wow," said Oliver. "You really do take this seriously!"
"Well we need to! It's called 'A Climate Emergency'," she said, looking him up and down. "Lots of designer gear, Olly!"
"Oh, God! How did I know this was going to lead to a ritual guilt trip session!" he joked. "Let's examine this rucksack for its environmentally friendly credentials!" he said, grabbing Florence's rucksack.
"Give it back now!" she commanded him.
"No!" he said, raising it about his head so it was out of her reach.
"If you don't give it back now, you're going to regret it!"
"Oh! She's like a Jack Russell Terrier, all bark and no bite!" he said, clearly trying to goad her.
"I'll give you one more chance not to be seriously embarrassed in front of your friends!"
"Ohhhh, she likes a challenge!" he continued, enjoying the opportunity to flirt with Florence.

Suddenly, in one swift move that was so fast it was hard to see, she took his legs out from under him. He fell backwards in the sand and she grabbed her ruck sack. As he groaned with the shock of what had just happened, she stood over him in triumph.

"Whoa!" screamed Mohammed. "Very impressive!"
"That was amazing!" said Nick, giving Florence a round of applause.
"Oh, thanks, don't worry about me and my dignity!" said Oliver, looking very sorry for himself.
"No, we won't!" said Mohammed. "You got what you deserved!"
"I have to say, I agree, Olly! Where the hell did you learn to do that, Florence?"
"Oh, lots of self defence lessons over several years. I discovered, much to my surprise, that I'm rather good at it!"
"Are you a black belt?" joked Mohammed, clearly not expecting an affirmative reply.
"Yes."
"OMG! I'm not going to mess with you!" he laughed.

Florence held her hand out to help Oliver back up. "I don't think so," he joked, holding his hands up in surrender. "You're dangerous!"

He eventually took her hand but instead of allowing her to help him up he pulled her down to the ground, catching her as she fell. "I've got you," he reassured her. "Kiss and make up? I think we're equal now!"
"Oh, ok!" she laughed, kissing him.

When Nick and Mohammed had wandered off to tell everyone about Oliver's ultimate humiliation, Oliver became more serious. "Did you take self defence lessons because of the attack?"
"Absolutely!" she said. "Hopefully, I will never have to use it to really defend myself but it makes me feel more secure that I can."
"You're very impressive! Not just because you're clearly talented and highly proficient but because you took the time to do this."
"I'm sorry I used it on you! That's never what it was intended for."
"Oh, I deserved it! You did warn me several times!"
"The look on your face and Mo and Nick's reaction does help to compensate for the hundreds of pounds I spent on lessons!"
"Oy, you," he said, pinning her down and tickling her until she laughed uncontrollably.

Over a drink in the bar, later that evening, the group discussed careers and ambitions.
"How did you get so much time off work, Nick?" asked Florence.
"Well, I had decided to resign and just get a new job on my return. There's a shortage of property solicitors in London with so much property development going on but when I handed in my notice the partners said they would hold my job open for 6 months so I have a job to go back to and won't have any hassle and time without a job on my return."

"They must think highly of you, Nick!" commented Florence.
"Well I hope so but it does engender loyalty. I'm not sure all law firms would be so forward thinking."
"How about you, Flo? What are you going to do?" asked Nick.
"I did some work experience with Unicef after university which I really enjoyed so I hope to work for an NGO or charity. Probably related to asylum seekers. They gave me the opportunity to go to 'The Jungle', a migrant camp, which was interesting but heart breaking. It was December and the conditions were horrendous. I was shocked!"
"Yes!" I've seen it on television," said Nick. "I agree that conditions aren't fit for human beings."
"Mind you," said Florence, "You have to admire the people there because they make the best of things. They divided roughly in to national groups and organised entertainment. I guess it is a case for birds of a feather flock together but there were talented people so it was a rich cultural experience. I loved the Syrian choir, the Afghan band and the Iraqi orchestra. I ended up helping them to organise a panto for the poor kids who had to endure the camp. It was great fun seeing their faces light up as they forget their hard lives. They could just be kids for a while which was very hard under normal circumstances. It was a highlight of my life."
"That is very moving, Flo! I can see why it had such a profound impact on you," said Nancy. "How about you, Olly?"

Oliver had been very quiet and seemed to be entranced by Florence's account of her work experience. Now, he looked distinctly uncomfortable. "Well, I can't beat Florence's work experience," he said, appearing to squirm in his seat."

"Oh, that doesn't matter, Olly. It's not a competition. Come on, you left university a few years before we embarked on this trip so you must have done something," commented Florence.

"Well," he said, "I did an internship with a marketing agency in London but I'm not sure that is what I want to do when I get back."

"Oh, come on, Olly!" said Mo. "Stop being so modest!"

Oliver glared at Mohammed. "Don't you remember me telling you not to mention it to Florence because she would think it was shallow and vain?" he said, angrily.

"Well, there's no going back now, Olly. We're intrigued," laughed Florence. "The mind boggles!"

"He's a male model," blurted out Mohammed.

"A male model!" exclaimed Florence, laughing.

"Yes! I knew you'd react like this which is why I didn't want you to know," he said, emphasising the last six words and continuing to glare at Mohammed.

"Have you been prancing down the cat walk?" laughed Nancy.

"Oh, what is this? Let's all have a good old laugh at Olly's expense?" he said, getting frustrated.

"No, seriously," said Florence, sensing his embarrassment and feeling sorry for him. "How did you get in to it?"

"Quite by chance. I didn't go out looking for a job as a model. Honest! When I was doing the internship at the ad agency they sent me out every day to get the sandwiches and drinks from the local cafe. They made sure I knew my place. Anyway, as I was walking there one day I was approached by a scout for a modelling agency who asked me if I wanted to be a model. I said no, obviously, and to be quite honest, I thought it was a scam but he wouldn't take no for an answer. I ended up giving him my contact details and the rest is history. I just did a few jobs. Photo shoots for magazines and catalogues and it paid for some of this trip."

"Here he is!" said Mohammed, gleefully, handing round pictures of Oliver, both individually and in embraces with beautiful female models, on his tablet.

"Oh, I give up!" moaned Oliver, looking at Florence so he could gauge her reaction. "And let's get it all out there, shall we? Full disclosure! My designer clothes were given to me by the modelling agency. A perk."

"Very attractive women," commented Florence, looking rather put out by seeing Oliver entwined with them.

"It's heavily airbrushed," he said, "those models aren't half as attractive in real life. They're unnaturally tall and skeletal. Not my cup of tea at all."

"I'm pleased to hear it!" laughed Florence, visibly relaxing. "I knew they were airbrushed because it doesn't look anything like you in the flesh!"
"Oh why do I feel as if I've just been through the wringer?"
They all laughed. "Come on, Olly!" said Nick. "Let's get the next round in! I think you probably need a drink!"
Once they had left, Florence and Nancy grabbed Mo's tablet to look at the photos again. "Well," said Nancy. "I said he was a good looking guy from day one!"
"You did," agreed Florence.

Day 79

The group quiz became a competitive affair. Nancy and Florence paired up; and Florence invited Angela and Fatima to join them but when she told Nancy she protested that she'd invited the boys to be part of the team. "No way," said Florence. "With Fatima on our side we're a dead cert'."
"But I think Olly's really clever," protested Nancy.
"No!" exclaimed Florence. "Olly's arrogant enough to think he's clever." She hadn't, however, seen Oliver standing behind her.
"Throwing the gauntlet down are we your ladyship?" he said, sarcastically.
"You bet!" smiled Florence.

"Come on Dave, let's get this show on the road!" shouted Mo.

"As I was saying," laughed David, "before I was rudely interrupted. No use of mobile devises or internet access is permissible during the quiz so please switch everything off now."

As the quiz got underway, Florence's team drew ahead with questions on history and literature but the music and geography rounds were great levellers. Florence groaned as the last round was chosen at random and turned out to be sport.
"Not so confident now, are you?" mouthed Oliver across the room to Florence who scowled before looking away.
Mohammed sang, "You're not laughing anymore!" at the top of his voice!

Oliver and the boys were in their element and even beat the girls' team when the questions were on women's sport. They celebrated loudly when they were declared the winners and patted each other on the back.

"Well that was embarrassing!" said Nancy with an 'I told you so tone'.
Florence tried to slip away but Oliver was lying in wait. 'Hang your head in shame for calling me arrogant!' said Oliver, surprising Florence from behind and enveloping her to nuzzle her right ear.
'Ok, I admit I underestimated you!'
'Oh, did I just get an apology from the high and mighty Ms Bloom?".

'Don't get too cocky for your own good Mr Fraser or you may trip over your own ego. Mind you, no change there!'
He twirled her round before she could protest and lifted her high in the air, before spinning her round. Against her better nature, she squealed with delight.

Nancy and Mo sat observing. Still finding it hard to get used to the idea of Florence and Oliver being friends, Mo commented, 'I think the iceberg has melted!'

When the group retired to the bar, Nancy slipped Florence her keys. "I won't be up for two hours," she told her. "I won't pretend I'm not jealous as hell!" she smiled at her but like you said earlier in this trip, I'm an old romantic!"
"Thanks, Nancy!" said Florence, hugging her.

"Nancy's letting us have the room for two hours so you can help me prep for the next quiz!" Florence whispered to Oliver.
"Wow! Good old Nancy!" he said. "Mind you, it may take more than two hours with general knowledge like yours!"
"Watch it, you!" she said, smiling.
"I need to pop back to my room. I'll see you there." said Oliver.

Oliver arrived at the room with a small container. "Simon's magic potion!" he said. "Your turn to give me a massage!"

As Florence massaged Oliver's back and shoulders, all the pain of grief and resulting depression seemed to melt away. The sensual feel of her hands gliding over his skin was luxurious and he felt deeply relaxed and sexually aroused in a way that he had never experienced. He had been able to dull the pain with alcohol, marijuana and masturbation but he'd never felt like this before. He sighed deeply before massaging Florence and making love to her.

"So marks out of ten for my massage," teased Florence who was lying on top of Oliver and stroking his hair. "Um, about a six I'd say!"
"A what!" she exclaimed, digging him in the ribs.
"I think you need more practise and I'm happy to be your test dummy!"
"You are a dummy if you think you can get away with that Oliver Fraser!" she said, smiling. "Now you need to get back to your own room, we don't want to abuse Nancy's kind gesture, do we?"
"That was never two hours! It felt like ten minutes. Can't I just swap with Nancy and share a room with you?"
"Now we both know that's not appropriate. Anyway, would you inflict Mo on poor Nancy?"
"There's nothing wrong with Mo!" said Oliver, "He's a great room mate!"

"Good! So go back to him! Now!" ordered Florence, before he turned her over and kissed her in order to silence her.

"Thanks for that! Nancy! It was wonderful!" said Florence.
"Well I just wanted to be able to finally say, 'I told you so, Florence!'"
"You did Nancy and I wish I'd listened to you. I was such an idiot. You once asked me why I disliked him so much. He reminded me of someone who raped me. It took me far too long to realise he's nothing like the man who raped me."
"Oh God, Florence." said, Nancy. "I don't know what to say."
"You don't need to say anything, Nancy. You've supported me in ways you will probably never know!" she said as she hugged Nancy.

Day 80

"Hurry up and finish your breakfast!" Florence told Oliver. "We're going to church."
"Why?" asked Oliver.
"There's a beautiful church on the opposite side of the square. I'll explain why when we get there."
"Has anyone ever told you that you're really bossy?"
"Yes! All the time," she replied, refusing to rise to his obvious insult.

The large square full of people coming and going was edged with attractive colonial buildings and there was an enormous equestrian statue in the middle. Huge trees with roots that snaked to the ground were home to chattering and screeching parrots that periodically dived and strove across the square. It was a kaleidoscope of colour and the square acted like an amphitheater to enhance the acoustics so that crying children and souvenir sellers who were far away could be heard clearly on the other side of the square. Oliver took Florence's hand and allowed her to guide him across the square. They were still getting used to the idea of being a couple but it felt good to be together like this and away from the rest of the group which they spent so much time with. Just the two of them.

As they entered the church via the ancient large wooden doors of the main entrance, the temperature difference hit them. It was cool and dark inside the cavernous church. There were a few elderly people with their heads bowed in prayer but generally it felt very deserted and empty.

Florence and Oliver sat about three rows back and soaked up the peaceful atmosphere. "Are you religious, Florence?"
"Not particularly," she replied, "but my Mum is and any opportunity we get, we light a candle for my granny who died a few years ago. I was very close to granny and I find it really comforting. That little bright light in the darkness is symbolic of her living on

in some way. It's hard to explain how and why. I feel as if she lives on if I keep her alive by talking about her too."
"Did she live near you?"
"Yes, just round the corner with my grandad who now lives with my Mum. She was a nurse for many years. She was also a collector. She had all sorts of collections around the house: Russian dolls, biscuit tins, old post cards. My mum and I used to make fun of her for it but now I realise it was what made her her; a passionate woman full of character."

"Are you religious?" Florence asked Oliver.
"That's a hard one," he said, welling up. "We always went to church when I was a child. With my mum in the diplomatic service, it is an important way of playing a part in the local expat community. It was kind of expected of my Mum, especially once she reached the level of ambassador. When Henry died, I think my parents got a lot of comfort from their faith but I'm afraid I just can't get my head around it. Initially, I couldn't reconcile what had happened to my twin with God. Why? I just asked why the whole time, looking skyward as if I was having a conversation with God. I got very angry at times and hated God. I really wish I could embrace the faith that my mum and dad have but I just can't. I guess I'm agnostic."

Florence took Oliver's hand and they sat in silence for a long time before she said, "Come on, let's light candles." Florence had coins in her hand which she put in the box and they listened to them clink in to place at the bottom. They each light a candle and placed them with the other flickering candles on the tray before returning to their seats.

"Thanks, Florence," said Oliver, squeezing her hand and gazing at the candle that he had light. "I can see why you find it comforting. I didn't even know what a light Henry was in my life until I lost him. He was just always there, from the dawn of time until that light was suddenly snuffed out." He broke off and stared at the ground, wiping away tears. "It made me realise that you shouldn't take anything for granted."

"How did you say goodbye to him?"
"You mean the funeral and memorial service?"
"Yes."
"So many people wanted to come that we had to have it in the cathedral. It's enormous but it was absolutely packed. The whole thing is a bit of a blur. I spent most of it asking why it was him rather than me in that coffin. I just wanted to die instead." Florence noticed that he tightened his hands in to fists and screwed up his face, clearly struggling to cope with his emotions and the tension. She gently rubbed his back as he slumped forward. "I felt scared and angry. It all just felt senseless and unfair. People were very kind and said wonderful things about Henry. They said he was in a better place but I just felt as if he had gone in to a black hole. The pain was overwhelming and I felt very

empty. We played his favourite songs and people read poems and psalms that reflected Henry. The funeral and memorial was just the start of a very long journey of healing. I'm still on it and I feel as if it will never end."

"Tell me a happy memory you have of Henry," said Florence.
Oliver paused and took a long time before he started to talk. He seemed to be playing it over in his mind before he relayed it to Florence. "We were staying in the French Pyrenees and we had mountain bikes at the house so we set off early with a picnic and lots of water to do a mountain bike trail. He was following the map but he managed to get us lost." Oliver broke off to laugh at the memory. "We spent ages trying to find the track again but in the end we just gave up and had our picnic. We'd smuggled out a few beers from dad's stash and the views were amazing. It was very relaxing just chilling together and chatting. Feeling relaxed is something I miss because I don't think I have ever fully relaxed since his death. We ended up ringing dad and he came and picked us up."
"Did your dad find out you'd stolen his beer?"
"No!" he laughed. "And he probably wouldn't have been too bothered but he wouldn't have wanted Mum to find out or we would all have been in trouble!"

"I've suffered from insomnia since Henry's death. I've had lots of treatment at sleep clinics but I still struggle to sleep well. This trip is the first time I've slept well in ages. I think all the fresh air and energetic hikes help as well as my Fairy God Mother."

"Your Fairy Godmother?" asked Florence, looking confused."

"You!" he said, laughing and pulling her close. They bowed their heads together, as if in prayer before Oliver said, "Come on, let's get lunch. My treat!"

They sat out in the warm sunny square and shared a selection of dishes, at times feeding each other with a new flavour or ingredient that they had found amongst the many colourful ceramic dishes arranged on the table.
"I could get used to this," smiled Florence.
"Me too!" said Oliver, taking her hand and kissing it. "You know what you said earlier about me being your Fairy God Mother? Well you're my Fairy God Father!"
Oliver smiled at her before adding, "My pleasure, but don't let Mo hear you calling me a fairy! He'll have a field day!"

"How come you drink like a fish?" said Obi to Mohammed when the group gathered later in the bar. "I thought Muslims weren't supposed to drink."
"They're not," said Mohammed, "but do I look like a Muslim who follows the rules?"
"So what do your parents say about that?"

"Oh God, they don't know. They'd kill me. They think I'm a good Muslim boy who goes to the mosque on a Friday and reads his Koran!"
"Yer, the Kings Head Mosque on York Road!" laughed Nick, closely followed by the Mosque Night Club."
"And my only reading material these days is Page 3 of the Sun!"
"They abolished that years ago!" remarked Florence, "So that's not true."
"No, I just go online these days!" laughed Mohammed. Then he seemed to become more serious. "But being serious for a moment, my parents are picking me up at Heathrow so all you Brits in the group had better keep your mouths shut!"
"What's it worth?" joked Oliver.
"Florence will have a chat with them! Won't you? Get your own back time."
Florence looked awkwardly at Nancy but the others didn't notice.

Once they were back in the room Nancy rounded on Florence. "You're going to have to tell him soon, Flo. It will only make things worse if you leave it."
"I know!" said Florence but I'm just not sure how to broach it. "What do I say? Oh, sorry Olly, I know we've become really close and I really care about you but I'm off to the other side of the world when we finish this trip. It was a great holiday romance, though!"
"Yer! I see what you mean when you put it that way."

"It wasn't as if it wasn't booked and organised even before we met!"

Day 82

Several days later, Florence and Oliver were snuggled up together in a coffee bar. She was reading her book and he was staring in to space.
"Penny for your thoughts." said Florence.
"Oh, I was just thinking about how happy I am. I'd forgotten what it was like to be happy."
"Me too!" she said. "We've both been through difficult times but now we have each other it's easier to push the black clouds away, I guess. But," she said, "I do have something I need to tell you."
"Is this about your trip Down Under?" he said, fixing her with a stare.
"How do you know about that?"
"Nancy slipped up a few days ago and let the cat out of the bag. I was wondering when you were going to tell me, young lady."
"You mean, I've been agonising about when to tell you for the last few days and you've known all along!"
"Yep!"
She punched him playfully on the chest and he pulled her close to him.
"I'm not going to pretend I won't miss you like mad but it's only six months. I'll be waiting for you at the airport when you return, welcome balloons in hand! You're only going for six months, aren't you?" he said, suddenly looking worried.

"Well!" she said, with a twinkle in her eye. "I might meet a tall and handsome stranger and fall in love. Who knows!"
"I think you've already done that!" he laughed.
"Oh, I always said you were arrogant and entitled," she laughed, kissing and hugging him.
"You won't ever leave me, will you?" Florence said.
"No, and I won't ever let you leave me. You might be off to Oz but I'll be checking up on you at least ten times a day!"
"Ditto", she laughed.

"When you get back from Australia, how about a trip to Paris?" asked Oliver. "Our first trip together. Well, I guess this is our first trip together, technically speaking, but you know what I mean, just the two of us."
"Sounds wonderful!" replied Florence.
"Have you ever been?"
"What to Paris? No Olly! Mum could hardly afford the rent, let alone trips to Paris."
"Oh, yer, sorry," he said, looking uncomfortable. "My parents used to 'drag' me round the galleries and museums of Europe and I really resented it but I'm starting to realise I was very lucky. I vaguely remember the Muse d'Orsay because it's in an old train station and the restaurant behind the station clock is pretty cool."
"Yes, I've seen pictures of it," replied Florence.
"We'll have to go there on our trip! Oh, and I'm an expert on Mondrian now! I'm not going to get caught

out like that again! I'm ashamed to say, I've seen his art work in Paris and I still didn't recognise it!"

"I had no idea I had unsettled you enough for you to go away and look him up!" Florence laughed. "You are competitive then!"

"Well, when it came to that sour faced you I used to know, yes!" he smiled.

Florence swiped at him and he playfully grabbed her arm. "Now if you do that, I won't come to Paris with you!" he joked.

Day 83

Florence woke up with a bad head and a stomach ache after a restless night. All she wanted to do was turn over and stay in bed but there was the Itinerary on the bedside table screaming out 'Best Art Gallery for Local and Indigenous Art' to her. She'd been looking forward to this and was reluctant to miss it.

"Are you ok, Florence?" asked Nancy.
"Not great, Nance but I'll be fine once I've had a few pain killers. You go on to breakfast and I'll come and find you."

Fifteen minutes later, Florence joined Nancy with a cup of coffee from the breakfast buffet.
"This should do the trick!" she said listlessly and unconvincingly. "Sorry to leave you on your lonesome."

"Oh, no problem," replied Nancy. "I'm just worried about you, but I did have some entertainment. Look over there."

Florence looked over to the other side of the dining room where Akemi had found some fellow Japanese travellers of a similar age. She was talking animatedly to them and smiling and laughing. To someone who didn't speak Japanese, it sounded like a flock of roosting starlings.

"That's great for Akemi," said Florence. "It must be a relief to speak her own language after all these weeks."
"Have you seen who's in the middle of them?" asked Nancy, conspiratorially.
"No," replied Florence, not feeling in the mood for riddles.
"Look closely!" ordered Nancy.
Florence looked more carefully and then spotted Oliver, chatting away to the group. He was clearly the centre of attention.
"Oh, yes!" said Florence. "He speaks Japanese."
"Does he?" asked Nancy, looking surprised. "Is there no end to his talents?"
"He lived there for a year as a kid."
"Oh, he's trying to make his excuses and says he needs to speak to his girlfriend. So it's official then!"
"I'm not sure, he's never called me his girlfriend before," said Florence.
Oliver took a selfie with the group and then headed in the direction of Florence and Nancy.
"He's coming over!" whispered Nancy.

"Could be either of us then!" joked Florence.
"In my dreams!" replied Nancy.

"Hello ladies," said Oliver, sitting down opposite Florence who was slumped forward with her head in her hands. "What's the matter, Florence?" asked Oliver, noticing she was unwell. "You look dreadful!"
"Oh, thanks, Olly," groaned Florence. "And a very good morning to you too!"
"Why aren't you in bed?"
"Because it's the gallery visit, you know, the one I've been really excited about."
"So?"
"So, I can't miss it."
"Yes, you can. You need to go back to bed."
"Don't tell me what to do!" said Florence sounding frustrated.
"Has she eaten anything, Nancy?"
"No and she's hardly touched her coffee. She woke up sick and has taken pain killers."
"I am here!" said Florence, sounding angry.
"Look Flo," said Oliver, brushing her hair back out of her face. "Come back to the room and we'll discuss it there. We've still got half an hour until the tour starts."
"No!" she said.
"Look, are you going to walk back to he room with me or do I have to carry you back? Do as you're told for once in your life!" he said, firmly.
"He's not going to take no for an answer, Flo! I get the impression he means it!" said Nancy.

"Oh, okay," she replied, "but I still want to go."

Once back at the room they lay on Florence's bed, Oliver with his arm around Florence.
"It wouldn't be fair on the others because you may be infectious!"
She became tearful as she realised that what he said made sense.
"Look, I'll go on the tour and I'll do extra research and then when it's our free day tomorrow, we can go to the gallery and I will be your guide. How does that sound?"
"Perfect!" she smiled. "Thanks, Olly! Mind you, let's hope you don't come down with my infectious disease!" she smiled.
"I'm immune!" he said, kissing her.

He sat and held her hand while she dosed off to sleep and the next thing she knew he was back with a large and illustrated guide to the gallery which he proudly handed to her.
"How are you feeling?" he asked, tenderly stroking her cheek.
"Much better, thanks! The sleep did me the power of good. I hate to say it but you were right!"
"I usually am!" he joked.
"How was the tour?"
"Really interesting and you did me a favour because Mo, Matt and Obi just headed straight for the cafe and didn't bother with the tour. and I would probably have

joined them until recently but I really enjoyed it. It was fascinating."
"Really?" asked Florence. "Are you sure you're not just saying that to impress me?"
"No!" said Oliver, looking offended.

Day 84
True to his word, Oliver took Florence to the gallery the next day and acted as her guide. In the ornate art nouveau cafe afterwards they discussed their favourite paintings. "I loved the landscapes, particularly the ones with the ancient sights incorporated in to them," said Oliver, smiling. "I still can't believe I'm taking an interest in art!"
"My favourite was the woman with the head of a man on a platter!"
"Are you trying to tell me something?" he joked. "Oh and in case you're trying to catch me out you're talking about Salome and the Beheading of St John the Baptist!" he said with an air of triumph.

Back in her room Florence told Nancy how impressive Oliver's tour had been.
"Well," said Nancy, "my spies tell me he was up half the night prepping for it but I was sworn to secrecy so don't you dare say anything."
"Your secret's safe with me!" laughed Florence.

Day 85
A crackly voice on the radio alerted David to a serious accident at the rock climbing site. "I need to get over

to the rock climbing area!" shouted David to Malcolm, the driver. "Sarah, you wait with the rest of the group." Florence had heard everything and felt sick with panic. She knew Olly was doing the most challenging section and couldn't contain her fear that something terrible had happened to him.
"I want to come with you," she told David.
"Are you sure? It may be traumatic for you."
"I don't care!" said Florence. "I'm coming!"
Malcolm drove faster than he normally did and on arrival at the site, Florence was horrified to see the blue lights of an ambulance flashing. Mohammed met them. "It's Olly!" he confirmed. He slipped and hit his head against the rock face. He's unconscious."
Florence gasped and jumped out of the bus.
Mohammed caught hold of her. "They won't let you in to the ambulance. I've tried. They're doing all they can."
David went to talk to the instructors and other members of the group.
"What happened?" asked Florence, clearly finding it hard to contain her emotions.
"It was a simple accident. Olly was pushing himself to the limit. You know he's an experienced rock climber and that he wants to challenge himself."
"Why?" she said, now starting to sob.
Mohammed put his arm around her and guided her to a seat. "We both know he's strong and fit. I'm sure he'll come through this. Try not to worry."
Suddenly, the ambulance put its sirens on and started to move.

Florence gasped and put her head in her hands.
David rushed over. "Don't worry, they've told me they are taking him to the local hospital as a precaution. Come on, let's follow."

When they arrived at hospital there was a long, tense wait for news. Florence paced up and down nervously and refused to be comforted by Mohammed.
Eventually, a doctor came to speak to them. "He has regained consciousness and the x-rays show no serious injury but we will need to keep him in overnight for observation. Hopefully, we will be able to discharge him tomorrow."
"Can we see him?" asked Florence. "Yes, but only for ten minutes because he needs to rest."

They made their way to his room where Oliver looked very pale and had a bandaged head."
"What the bloody hell did you think you were doing?" shouted Florence, angrily.
Hey, Florence!" said Mohammed, clearly surprised, "Calm down."
"Don't tell me to calm down!"
"Good to see you too, Flo," said Oliver, sheepishly.
You really scared me!" she said, hugging him round his middle so as not to get near his injured head and sobbing again.
"I know. I'm sorry" he said, stroking his hair. "I knew you'd give me a bollocking!" he joked.
"Don't you ever do that to me again."
"Yer, you're not James Bond!" joked Mohammed.

David, who had been talking to the doctor, entered the room. "Good to see you're awake again, Olly. You had us all worried there. The doctor says you need to rest and you can leave hospital tomorrow."
"Thanks, David."
"Ok, Guys, we'd better leave him to get some sleep."
"I'm not going anywhere!" said Florence. "I'm staying right here."
"Oh, for goodness sake!" said David, "I'll go and see what the doctors say."
"She wants to check you don't go off with that cute nurse!" joked Mohammed but soon checked himself as Florence looked up and glared at him. When she had buried her head in Oliver again they both exchanged 'we'd better watch ourselves because she's on the war path' looks.
David returned. "Well the doctor said you can stay so long as you don't stop him sleeping. Are you sure about this Florence?"
"Absolutely!"
"Well we'll be back at 8 am tomorrow morning but you've got my number if you need me. My phone will be on all night."
"Thanks, David," said Florence.
Have a good night's sleep, Olly."
"Thanks! I'll try."

Once they had gone Oliver and Florence held hands and gazed at each other.
"I thought I'd lost you for a moment there," she said.

"You're not getting rid of me that easily, my love!" he laughed.
"Now get some rest!" she said. "Florence's orders."
And with that he closed his eyes and slept.

Day 86

David arrived at the hospital at 8 am and the doctor checked Oliver's head and blood pressure, and declared that he was fit enough to be discharged.

"How are you feeling?" asked David.
"I've got a splitting head ache but other than that, I'm fine!"
"He's just playing for sympathy now!" joked Florence.
"Oy, watch it you!" laughed Oliver, handing her his bag to carry.

Back at the hotel, everyone was keen to check Oliver was better and hear about the accident. He retold what had happened and how he had no actual memory of banging his head.
"Oh, I can help him fill you in on that one," said Mohammed.
"Not at the moment you can't! Come on Oliver, you need to get some rest," said Florence.
"Oliver, ay, only my mum calls me that when I'm in trouble."
"Well you will be if you don't come to the room and get your head down," smiled Florence.

They left Mohammed dramatising the events of the day before.

About an hour later, Mohammed arrived at the room where Florence and Oliver were dozing.
"You need to go back to your own room and sleep, Flo! I need a bit of man to man time with Olly. Don't look at me like that!" he said firmly.
Florence got up and did as she was told. At the door she turned and said, "Good job you didn't get hurt Mo, I would never have forgiven myself."

She left, leaving Mo looking confused. "What did she mean by that?" he asked.
"I think she's trying to tell you she's your secret benefactor," laughed Oliver.
"You're kidding me!" exclaimed Mohammed. "I always said it was me she has the hots for and not you Mate!" he laughed.

Later that day, Florence went back to see Oliver. "Do you feel up to a trip to the coffee bar?"
"Sure," he said, "It will be good to blow out the cobwebs.
They were soon settled in a cosy corner. "Have you taken you tablets yet?" she asked him.
"Oh, stop it!" he joked. "I rang my parents earlier and I've already had that from my Mum. She's over protective."
"Well, it's hardly surprising!" said Florence. "Under the circumstances, I think she's allowed to be."

"Yes, I know you're right but it is an issue. She wraps me up in cotton wool even though I'm in my twenties now. My dad's told her it's not fair but she just can't help herself. I really do get that but I've got my own issues to deal with."

Day 87

Florence was making her way through the hotel lobby to breakfast when she was accosted by Oliver who had just jogged in to the hotel, puffing and panting. He hugged her tight and kissed her. "Get off me!" she said, sounding irritated. "You're all hot and sweaty!"
"I thought that's how you liked me!"
"Not at 8 in the morning!" she said, unable to stifle a smile. "Go and get a shower and shave before you come near me again!"

When Oliver joined Florence a little later, he had put on copious amounts of Mohammed's after shave.
"Will I do now?" he joked.
"I think you've over done it a bit!" said Florence.
"There's no pleasing some people!" he said, putting jam on the end of Florence's nose to annoy her.
"How old are you?" she asked, sarcastically. "Twenty three, going on thirteen!"
"Twenty four," said Oliver.
"I thought you were twenty three," said Florence.
"No, twenty four," he said, sounding a little flustered.
"No, you definitely said you were twenty three two weeks ago."

"Well, I was," he replied.
"Hang on a minute, so you've had a birthday and didn't tell anyone."
"Correct," he said.
"Why on earth not?"
"Because I don't celebrate my birthday."
"Oh, I see," said Florence, suddenly realising that it would also have been the birthday of his twin brother. "I'm really sorry!"
"That's okay, it's just hard."

A little later, Florence found Oliver with two small cupcakes. "I hope this won't upset you but one is for you and one if for Henry. Small steps. You eat Henry's and I'll eat yours," she said, pushing it towards him. She licked his provocatively to distract him and he smiled and ate the cupcake.

Later that evening, Oliver and Mohammed went to the bar. "If Florence has banned you from ever going rock climbing, does that mean our rock climbing trip to the Peak District is off?" asked Mohammed.
"Are you kidding?" laughed Oliver. "I thought it was me that was inexperienced when it came to women? Florence thinks she's the boss but 'what she doesn't know about, she doesn't care about'. Anyway, she's off to Australia for six months so we can get a lot of rock climbing in during that time! 'While the cats away, the mice will play'".
"Nice!" said Mohammed. "Good to see you're not scared of her!"

"Oh, I wouldn't go that far! If she ever found out I'd be petrified!" joked Oliver.

Day 88

Florence went to Oliver and Mohammed's room to ask whether they wanted to come in to the town with her and Nancy.

"He's not here," said Mohammed. "He asked me to tell you he's, now let me get this right, that he's gone to watch birds, he finds it relaxing."

"What?" asked Florence, looking confused and irritated.

"Oh no, sorry!" said Mohammed. "That's what he asked me not to say," he continued, clearly enjoying clowning around with Florence. "Now what was it, he's gone bird watching with his binoculars, he finds it relaxing. It's a hobby of his."

"Oh," said Florence. "I didn't know that."

"What are your hobbies, Florence?"

"I've got lots," she smiled, "most of which I couldn't possibly share with you, Mo!" she said, getting her own back.

"Do you fancy talking about the clean ones for my vlog?"

"Ok," said Florence, "I'll catch up with you later."

"Oh there you are!" said Florence, finding Oliver concealed behind a large potted rubber plant at the far end of the hotel lounge with his book. "I've been looking all over for you."

"I'm hiding from Mo whose trying to get me to be interviewed for his vlog!"
"Why have you got a problem with that?" asked Florence.
"Because, obviously, I'm sick and tired of him sticking a camera in my face to get reactions."
"I don't understand why you're making such a big deal of it."
"You don't have to share a room with him! He was trying to film me the other day when I was cleaning my teeth in my boxer shorts!"
"Well I've agreed to be interviewed," said Florence and he's heading over here after he gets me a coffee.
"Oh, you are kidding me, Flo! Why are you encouraging him? He already thinks he's Luton's answer to Quentin Tarantino!"
"As you're always saying to me, stop being so uptight. What harm can it do? It's not as if he has a following of millions!"
"I think he's got thousands of followers. Well, that's what he's told me."
"Are you sure that's not just him exaggerating? You know, wishful thinking and all that? Have you looked at it?"
"No! Why would I want to watch the bloody thing?"
"Are you not just a little bit curious?
"No, absolutely not!"
"What's it called?"
"Mo in Motion, I think. Not a good start!"
"Oh!" exclaimed Florence. "He wasn't joking! He's got a following of thousands!"

"Has he?" asked Oliver, looking surprised. "Oh, here he comes!"

"Alright, Olly. I guess Florence has told you that she has agreed to be interviewed!" said Mohammed.

"She has and no, I'm not going to be next."

"Well don't worry, the last time she was in my vlog, she got way more 'likes' than you do."

"She's been in one of your vlogs?"

"Oh yes, several, haven't you, Florence."

"You never told me, Florence!" said Oliver, looking disconcerted.

"I don't have to give you a run-down of everything I do, Olly!" she said, smiling and clearly enjoying his discomfort. "Ok, Mo, shall we get on with this?"

"So, Florence, as we come to the end of our Gap Year Trip, please tell us about your highlights."

"Well there have been many! Where do I start? We've travelled through an eclectic mix of environments and eco systems and so many of the views on our hikes have just taken away my breath. But the highlight for me has been the amazing people I've met on this trip who I hope will be friends for life." At this point she made eye contact with Oliver who had been trying to resist the temptation to listen with little success. "Take Mohammed here," she continued, "he has been so inspired by the beauty of the landscape that he has committed to a major change in lifestyle." Mohammed looked very confused at this point. "He has committed himself to become a climate change activist and to practise what he preaches. His vlogs next year will feature the Climate Change Protest Marches he goes on and his new life style which will see him cut out single use plastic and improve recycling." Mohammed looked horrified.

"You know that I'm just going to edit out that bit!" he said.
"Well if you do that then I won't be in your vlog again and like you said, I get lots of 'likes'," said Florence, smiling.
"Well, I think you've just scored an own goal, Mate!" laughed Oliver.
"There's still time to change your mind, Olly!" said Mohammed, ignoring his sarcasm. "Ok, where's Nancy. She's next!"

The group had clubbed together to pay for Mohammed to join them on an afternoon of mountain biking. They collected their bikes from a hut and wound their way up a steep mountain trail with stunning views across vegetation clad mountains whose tops were bathed in clouds. Colourful birds shrieked in the tree tops and they narrowly missed a large lizard who was plodding across the track.

At the top of the pass they stopped for a picnic lunch. "Well this beats going down the park on my bike with my mates back home. Thanks guy!" said Mohammed. "I owe, you!"

Later that day, on the steep ride back down the mountain, Mohammed came careering past Oliver and Florence shouting, "Look out! My breaks have failed!"
He disappeared round the corner and out of sight.
"Oh my God!" shouted Florence, panic in her voice.
"Oh, he's just messing around! You know what he's like!" said Oliver but when they rounded the corner there was no sign of Mohammed.
They both stared in horror at the steep drop. Florence gasped and Oliver grabbed her around the waist, worried she was about to faint.

At that point they heard laughter coming from a bush on the other side of the path. Oliver pulled Mohammed unceremoniously out of the bush, threatening to throw him over the edge for playing such a cruel joke. He noticed Mohammed had his phone out. "I hope you haven't been filming!" he exclaimed.
"Don't ever do that again, Mo! It's NOT funny!" said Florence, sternly.

The bikes didn't need to be back for another hour so Florence and Oliver stopped on a rocky bluff overlooking the dramatic views of the valley below and mountains rising up like a fan around them. They sipped from their water bottles and ate the fruit still left from the picnic lunch. The rest of the group had gone on to the bottom of the trail so they had the world to themselves and they felt as if they were wrapped in it.

They just sat without saying anything for about five minutes but then Florence asked, "What are you thinking about?" She already knew the answer. She hadn't known Oliver for very long in the grand scheme of things but the intensity of their relationship and the fact that she had opened up her soul to him more than anyone else in her entire life meant that she had quickly learnt to reading his moods and emotions.
"Henry," he said, simply. "Looking at this view makes me wonder if he is in this kind of heaven."
"Was he buried or cremated?" asked Florence.
"He was cremated. There's a small plaque in a local graveyard next to my granddad. I go and sit with him and talk to him for hours. It does really help to have somewhere to go but it just seems so wrong. He's there with all these people that lived to old age, as it should be. There is a baby but apart from that Henry is the only child, someone who never got to be an adult and experience all the highs and lows that go with that."
"Does he answer you?" asked Florence.
Oliver buried his head in his hands and sobbed.
Florence gently stroked his hair and he lent his head on her shoulder. "You don't have to answer," whispered Florence.
"No," he eventually stuttered. "It helps to talk about it. Sometimes I can hear his voice in my head but..." he trailed off, "not always."
"What would he say now?" asked Florence.
"Oh, he'd be pulling my leg! We used to make fun of each other all the time. He'd be with Mo and Nick at

the end of the trail and make fun of us with them when we turn up late!" he smiled squeezing her hand.
"Yer!" he said, as if he was picturing the scene.
"Oh," said Florence, looking at her watch. "We'd better get going!"
"No!" he said, taking her head in his hands and stroking her hair. "Let's give them all something to talk about!" He kissed her and she closed her eyes as she felt his moist lips kissing hers. It was a long, sensual experience that drew them closer together.

They free wheeled down the rest of the trail and were greeted by the cheers and shouts of the rest of the group. Oliver did and emergency stop next to Mohammed and Nick, spraying them with grit and sand. They swore at him and pushed him off his bike. Mohammed sprayed him with water from his water bottle.
"Oh, that's so childish!" commented Florence. "How old are you lot?"
"Ohhhh!" they trilled, sarcastically before spraying Florence with water. She swore at them and walked off, not wanting them to see the smile forming on her face.

Later, Oliver and Florence sat in the hotel grounds having coffee. "I'm looking forward to the carnival tomorrow night," said Florence.
"Yes, so am I," replied Oliver. "It's very famous for being the biggest party in town! I've got an invitation

for us to see it from a balcony at the British Embassy because it goes right past."
You've what?" asked Florence, looking quizzically at him.
"Just what it says on the tin!" replied Oliver, sarcastically.
"Oh well if that isn't pulling strings, I don't know what is!"
"I didn't pull any strings."
"Yes, but you wouldn't get an invite unless you knew people in powerful places! Not what you know but who you know. Typical. Well I'm not coming."
"Oh for God's sake. Why do you have to get all high and mighty about it? Don't come if your principles won't allow it but I'm going," he said, walking off before stopping and adding, "and so is everyone else so you'll be left here all on your own."

"Grr!" groaned Florence through gritted teeth. She found Nancy in their room, painting her nails. "Are you going to see the carnival at the embassy, Nance?" asked Florence.
"I certainly am!" chimed Nancy. Oliver checked that it was ok for other passport holders to go. I'm really excited. "You'd never get in to a function at the U.S Embassy in a million years!"
"Most people wouldn't get in to the British Embassy unless they know the right people," replied Florence. "What are you going to wear?"
"I've told him I'm not going."

"You've what? Why?" asked Nancy, looking incredulous.

"Well it all sounded a bit like power and privilege to me but that was before I realised the rest of you were going."

"Well you'll have to come! You can't go to the carnival on your own. It wouldn't be safe."

"Oh great!" sighed Florence. "I need to post some cards. I'll see you later."

As Florence walked through the hotel she met Simon.

"Hello gorgeous!" he said. "I'm looking forward to seeing you in your cocktail dress and tiara tomorrow for the embassy. I'll do your hair and makeup."

"I've told Olly I'm not going!" said Florence.

"Why on earth have you done that?"

"Well I didn't realise the rest of you were going to wholeheartedly embrace the idea! Now I've backed myself in to a corner."

"Oh just go and tell him you've changed your mind."

"Oh, he'll love that!"

"I'm sure he'll just be pleased you're going. Go and find him now and tell him. He's in the lounge reading."

"Ok! Probably best to get it over with. Thanks, Simon!"

Florence found Oliver near the entrance to the hotel lounge and slipped on to the bench seat next to him."

"Look, Olly, I'm sorry. I'd love to come to the embassy tomorrow," she said, feeling herself go crimson.

"I didn't catch that," he replied, without looking up from his book.

"Yes, you did!" she said, snatching the book out of his hands and digging him in the ribs. "If you think I'm going to grovel, you can think again!"

"I knew you'd come round to the idea! Come here," he smiled, pulling her close and kissing her.

"Oh, yer! What made you so confident?"

"I asked Simon to have a word with you. I guessed you wouldn't be able to resist his charms."

"You did what?" she laughed. "Hang on a minute. How long have you known about this invite?"

"Um," he paused, trying to workout how much he could get away with. "About two weeks."

"About two weeks?" said Florence, looking incredulous. "And what about the others?"

"Um!" said Oliver, looking sheepish. "About two weeks!"

"You're kidding me! So why did I only find out today?"

"Why do you think? So I could get them all on side and close down your options!"

"Why didn't anyone else mention it to me?"

"Because I asked them not to say anything. We knew you'd be awkward and they want you to come as much as I do."

"You devious bastard!"

"Now, now! Less of the bad language! You don't want to end up apologising to me twice in one day!" Florence got up to leave. "Where are you going?" he asked.
"To deal with Simon, Nancy, Fatima, Nick and Mo!" she replied, sarcastically.
"Tell Simon I'll get him that drink I owe him tonight!" he shouted after her, gleefully.

Day 89

When Florence and Nancy went down to meet the rest of the group in the hotel reception, they realised that the men had hired tuxedos for the evening. "Oh! I think I've died and gone to heaven!" oozed Nancy. "I just love a man in a tux!" With that she immediately plunged in to the middle of the group.

Florence, focussed on Oliver who was talking animatedly to some of the other women in the group. She suddenly felt rather overwhelmed and light headed so sat down on the nearest sofa to recover. This trip had been transformative for Florence and her relationship with Oliver had developed very quickly. Was it too fast? Sometimes she felt as if she was in a dream and that she was going to wake up and be back in her room at university, sobbing after the attack and realisation of what had happened.

Why would someone with his vivacious personality and good looks even glance sideways at her? Someone who was soiled, dirty and disgusting. The rape had only lasted about five minutes, a conclusion that Florence had had to work hard with police investigators to come to because it had felt like much longer, but it was five minutes that had robbed her of her self worth. It was five minutes that had taken away her zest for life. It was five minutes that had given her years of anguish, mental health problems and anorexia. Five minutes that had robbed her of all her self confidence. It occurred to her that the previous weeks could have been an elaborate plot humiliate her for her terrible behaviour towards him in the early months of the trip.

Suddenly, she saw Oliver advancing towards her. "There you are! What are you doing over here?" he asked her. "I was hoping you wouldn't be able to keep you hands off me in my tux! I wanted to surprise you!"
"I'm speechless!" she said, trying to hide her insecurities.
"You look beautiful!" he said, taking her hands and stepping back to look at her. "Simon's done a good job!"
"Thank you, Olly!" she said. "Thanks for everything."
"Are you sure you're okay?" asked Oliver, looking concerned. "You're not still having second thoughts about coming?"
"Oh, no! It's just that when I start to feel happy I can't help letting dark thoughts in to my head that I can't get rid of."

"I know!" he replied. "Me too. An hour doesn't go by without me seeing Henry's head on that pavement with blood trickling out of his mouth," he said, looking at the floor and before quickly adding, "I'm sorry, I shouldn't have told you that. I don't want to burden you too."

"No," said Florence, stroking the side of his face. "I'm glad you did."

"We're in this together and we need to support each other," said Oliver.

Florence started crying. "Stop that! You'll mess up Simon's handiwork. Deep breaths! Now come on you, let's go and join the others. I need you by my side to make sure this embassy trip goes well," he said, wiping away her tears and leading her to the rest of the group, squeezing her hand as they went.

Florence, for her part, started to feel more relaxed, safe and secure.

"Well, helloooo, Ms Money Penny!" said Mo, approaching them with dark glasses on. "Mine's a martini, shaken not stirred. Do you want to see my gadgets?"

"Oh, yes!" joked Florence. "Does it include your ejector handle?" she said, winking at him.

"Oh for goodness sake! Will you two behave."

"Later!" said Mo, winking back, "not in front of the children!" he smiled, nodding at Oliver.

"We need to check on the taxis, Florence!" said Oliver, sounding irritated.

When they were out of earshot, Oliver said, "Why do you encourage him, Flo?"
"Oh, chill out Olly, anyone would think you were jealous," she replied, jokingly but his response surprised her.
"Well I am! Girls always go for the funny ones and in the comedy department I can't compete with Mo."
She noticed that he did look unsettled.
"Oh, don't be ridiculous, Olly! Me and Mo? Are you kidding? Mo's lots of fun but you're the only one for me!"
"Nice bit of rhyming there!" he smiled, looking more relaxed.

The group got taxis to the embassy through crowded and frenetic streets. When they entered they had their passports checked but once inside the hallway they were stood in front of an impressive neoclassical marble staircase. A woman in her early sixties came to greet them. "Olly!" she said, hugging him warmly, "It's so good to see you."
"And you, Aunty Stephanie! I haven't seen you for ages!"
"Yes, far too long," she replied, "but when your Mum said my favourite godson was passing through, I couldn't let you do that without having you over. Hugh is around somewhere. He's dying to see you too."
"Thanks for having my friends over as well"

"It's our pleasure and perfect timing with the carnival on tonight. I've reserved you a private room with a balcony and there are snacks and drinks in there."
"Wow!" replied Oliver. "That's amazing! Oh, and this is Florence, my girlfriend!"
Florence was still recovering from the revelation that the woman was Oliver's godmother and stuttered something about being pleased to meet her. She embraced Florence warmly.
"Your Mum didn't mention Florence!" observed Stephanie.
"That's because she doesn't know!" smiled Oliver. "We only met on this trip."
"Well I feel honoured!" smiled Stephanie. "Listen, I need to speak to some other guests but make yourselves at home and I'll catch up with you in a little while. But before I go, let's have a photo!"

Once Stephanie had disappeared, Florence rounded on Oliver. "You could have warned me she's your godmother."
"Oh and get more agro!" he replied. "I did't know she was going to announce it in front of you."
'Is she the ambassador?"
"No. She's married to him. Nice guy. He's Henry's godfather."
"Oh, I see!" said Florence. "You're all very close then."

The group made their way up to the first floor where they found a buffet, beer, wine and soft drinks. "This

is fantastic, Mate!" said Mohammed. "I promise not to get too drunk and be sick on that expensive shag pile carpet!" he joked.
"Don't you dare!" replied Oliver.

It wasn't long before they could hear the sound of the carnival drums. From their vantage point, they could watch large colourful flags billowing, enormous banners that sparkled with sequins, dancers in large feather head dresses and huge floats go by. Oliver stood behind Florence with his arms round her waist and they danced and gyrated rhythmically to the beat of the music which went on late in to the night.

Day 90
The next morning, Florence woke up next to Oliver. What am I doing in here?" she asked sleepily. You fell asleep and I had to carry you back. Simon let Mohammed sleep in his room. I think he still feels guilty!"
"So he should! And so should you!" she smiled.
"Well I was hoping to make amends before we go to breakfast," he smiled, sheepishly, pulling her close and caressing her.
"Is that what you call it?" she joked.
His phone beeped. "Just ignore that! It'll be my Mum. Steph sent her the photos she took of us! I'm just ignoring her at the moment!"
"That's mean!" laughed Florence. "Is that what you do to me?"

"Absolutely not, now come here! Let's do some more gyrating!" he laughed, pulling her close.

Later in the day, Florence and Oliver were sat with Fatima chatting about life before the trip. "You got arrested?" exclaimed Oliver, looking incredulously at Florence.
"Yes," she said, in a matter of fact tone.
"What for?" he asked, unable to stop his mouth falling open.
"Obstruction," she replied. "Friends and I were camping in central London during the two week protests and we sat on an approach road to the airport. The police were called. They tried to persuade us to move and when that didn't work there was a stand-off for about an hour. Then the order to physically remove us came through and they gave us a final warning but when we continued to refuse to budge they picked us up and physically moved us to the side of the road where we were handcuffed and put in a police van. I was at the police station for hours and my poor Mum was beside herself. In the end, I was given a caution and released. I remember this police officer telling us they would press charges if we were arrested again."
Florence held her phone out to show Oliver and Fatima a photo of the protest."
"You've got green hair!" exclaimed Oliver, continuing to look surprised at Florence's account of her exploits.

"So?" she said, sounding irritated and cocking her head to one side to fix him with a stern gaze. "Does that bother you?"
"No!" he replied, sounding flustered. "I just, oh I'm not sure..." he trailed off.
"So how did you feel about being arrested?" asked Fatima, coming to Oliver's rescue and drawing Florence's attention away from him.
"Angry!" she replied, firmly. "I guess I was furious with authority and the police for not prosecuting the man who raped me. Extinction Rebellion was a perfect way to channel my pent up anger. I've always been interested in environmental issues and the work of Green Peace so this was a good way to get involved and do some good in this world. It took my mind off things, the mental torture I'd been putting myself through, and I felt part of something really worthwhile. It was a great two weeks. There was a real sense of camaraderie and we spent hours singing and chanting. Oh, I know there has been lots of criticism of the protests but I get so frustrated by the way governments just sit back and do nothing."
"I agree!" said Fatima. "There needs to be major changes at the highest level and it just isn't happening. Sub-Saharan Africa, where I'm from, is at the front line of climate change. Harvests are failing and this is causing conflict between local tribes and even starvation in extreme cases."
"My Mum supports a charity that organises peanut based packs for malnourished children," said Oliver, suddenly looking more confident and less out of his

depth. "I've never really asked her much about it but you two have made me realise I need to show more interest," he mused.

"I'm looking forward to meeting your Mum!" said Florence. "It sounds as if we may have much in common!"

"Oh you do!" joked Oliver. "Like you, she's always on my case!"

Day 91

Oliver and Florence were under a huge and impressive tree that acted like a parasol to protect them from the fierce rays of the tropical sun. Oliver was lying length ways with his head on Florence's lap and she was stroking his hair.

"I see the girls have gone to museums and churches and the boys have gone on a bar crawl today!" said Florence.

"Well the girls are just swots!" joked Oliver.

"So, I'm guessing your weren't a swot at school then."

"Are you kidding? As far as I was concerned, school was for playing sport. I did pretty well at that but when it came to the academic side, I never really got that. Listening to you and Mo talking about school, I realise now how lucky I was and that I squandered my chances but you don't get that as a teenager."

"Did you ever get in to trouble?"

"Oh, yes! I remember Henry, myself and a gang of friends got hauled in to the Head Teacher's office for playing poker. I was very good at it and made a

fortune but he soon put a stop to it by threatening to contact our parents if we were caught again. On other occasions I got in to trouble for not doing homework or not being focussed and got a few detentions but Henry would do them for me if I had a cricket match."
 He paused and smiled at this memory. "I think the P.E. staff knew what we were up to but the other teachers never worked it out. I'd do detentions for him in return. We had plans to share a driving licence in the future. Whoever passed first was going to let the other use the licence. It sounds mad now but we were very excited about the prospect as teenagers."

"How do you get on with your sister? How old is she?" asked Florence.
"Lucy's two years younger than me and we've found it hard to work out how to relate to each other since the death of Henry. She used to be just the silly little sister who we'd tease mercilessly. Looking back we were really mean to her and picked on her. Henry's death hit her as hard as the rest of the family. One of her ways to deal with it in the first year after Henry died was to keep calling me Henry as if she could bring him back in me. I had some big slanging matches with her about it and my mum and dad had to get involved. We both had to have serious counselling and I realise now that we were each hurting in our own way and drowning in grief. We have started to come out of it and spend some time together, just the two of us.
 After all, we're both in our twenties now and I have started to realise that I miss one sibling to the extent

that it's a constant ache but I do have another sibling and I should value that. She once got delayed coming home from university on the train. Her phone was out of charge so she didn't let us know. I went in to a blind panic and that really made me think about what it would be like to lose her too, and that she was more precious to me than I ever realised."
"Wow!" said Florence. "That's really moving. You're lucky to have a sibling. I'm an only child and I envy friends who have got a brother or a sister. My Mum and I are very close and that may not have been the case if I had had a sibling. Who knows?"

"Do you ever wish you could get the rape case reopened?" Oliver asked Florence.
"Oh, yes!" she replied, "A day doesn't go by without me having visions of him in the dock being sentenced for what he did. A woman police officer who was trained to support rape victims looked me in the eye and said she believed me. That meant a lot to me. It really did because I know she believed me. I've written my Victim Impact Statement a million times in my head. It starts by describing how he violently over powered me and ignored my pleading for him to stop. It describes how he arrogantly denied it when we both know what happened on that night and how he is happy to imply I'm a liar. It ends with the impact he's had on my mental health, the torturous thoughts and most of all that damage he's done to my relationships with others, particularly other men."
She squeezed Oliver's hand.

"Well I think you're incredibly brave," he said, holding her tightly.
"Am I? Like you, I didn't choose this. I just had to deal with it."
"Do you worry that he will do it to someone else?" asked Oliver.
"Oh, yes! All the time and history suggests he will at some point."
"Give me his name. I'll kill him for you."
"Yes, I know you would," she said, putting her head on his shoulder, "which is why I won't ever be giving you his name!"

"Oh, I need to go. I'm off to meet up with the girls at the museum. Do you want to come too?" she asked.
"I'm afraid I have other plans," he laughed.
"Oh, don't tell me! Let me guess! Does it involve a bar crawl?"

When Florence met up with the boys in the early evening, the first thing that she noticed was that the table was full of empty beer bottles and the second thing she noticed was their slurred speech. "Having a good time, I see guys!" she said.
"Florence!" screeched Mohammed loudly. "Give us one of your crazy quotes!" he slurred, drunkenly.
"Oh, how about 'Hell is empty and all the devils are here' Prospero in the Tempest!"
"Oh stop being so pretentious, Flo!" said Oliver.
"Oh, you can tell you're drunk, Olly! You don't stand up to Florence when you're sober!" said Nick.

"Oh, perfect timing for 'Let's kill all the lawyers' Henry VI" joked Florence.

"I think she's taking the piss now! We must be able to think of one good quote to chuck back at her between us," moaned Mohammed.

"Now's the time we could really do with some quotes from 'A Taming of the Shrew'" joked Oliver.

"But, ironically, you can't summon up any so now is the perfect time to go to the bar and get me a drink!" laughed Florence.

Day 92

At breakfast, Mohammed entered the restaurant with Oliver looking triumphal and headed straight for Florence who was sat with Angela.

"Come, come, you wasp; i' faith, you are too angry." Mohammed said to Florence.

Angela looked confused but Florence smiled. "If I be waspish, best beware my sting."

"I warned you she'd be ready for you, Mo!" said Oliver.

Mohammed sneaked a look at a piece of paper, "My remedy is then, to pluck it out."

"That's cheating, Mo. You need to be spontaneous!" Florence chided.

"Um! I think you could be on to something here. I may chuck a few quotes in to make my vlog more culturally relevant! It could give a big boost to my likes! Let's chat later!"

The final long bus journey was imminent and David called a meeting after dinner to discuss safety issues. He began by telling them it was a serious safety briefing. "I don't want to worry you but there are credible reports about bandits operating in the area in the last few weeks. We had a tour bus ambushed last year and it was a frightening experience. Both Sarah and I lived through it and it is not an experience we want to repeat. The company has tightened up its procedures since then and the chances are that we will pass through the area without incident but it is important to prepare you just in case. Tomorrow morning, all your valuables will go in the hold. That includes mobiles, computers, jewellery and travel documents."
"What about my travel vlog? I need to post for my adoring fans every day."
"I'm afraid that if you don't take this seriously Mo, you will have to fly up to the coast and meet us there." said David sternly.
"Oh, ok, sorry David. I get the message," said Mohammed, feeling as if he'd been told off by a teacher at school.
The hold on the bus will be locked before we leave and we don't take a key. There is a duplicate key at the destination where we will be able to get access to the hold again. You all need to take the equivalent of $5 to give to any bandits. They know the drill. They're

poor farmers so they are likely to be armed with machetes. If we comply and give them money, we will all come out of this safe and well."
"Has anyone got any questions?"

"With my solicitor's hat on," said Nick, "I don't remember this in the Booking Details."
"I can assure you that it is buried in there, Nick. The company's legal team were crawling all over this one after the last incident happened. I wasn't involved at the point of booking and I could have scared you all at the start of the trip to the extent that it plays on your mind throughout but I decided the best course of action is to have this meeting and talk you through the salient points of what could happen but probably won't. Listen, I don't want you to have a sleepless night. Hopefully, this time tomorrow, we will be safely at our destination and laughing about all this. Ok, so if there are no more questions, enjoy the rest of the evening and I'll see you all tomorrow at 8am. I'm around if anyone wants to have a chat."

"Well, I think I need a drink after that," said Oliver.
"Me too," agreed Mohammed.

Day 93
The next morning everyone was at the bus by 8am and all the valuables were stashed below the bus and locked away. They boarded but Chloe had to ask

David to retrieve the key from reception to get her cash out.

They set off and bright sunshine made most of them drowsy. Florence enjoyed the stunning mountain scenery before dozing off on Oliver's shoulder. Several hours passed and they relaxed, forgetting about the threat of bandits. They had a pleasant picnic lunch and then boarded the bus to continue the long journey.

"Anyone fancy a sing song?" asked Nancy. "It's like the good old days, before we had mobiles and everyone started staring at screens."
"It's great!" agreed Florence. "I know the internet was an amazing invention but my Mum always claims it has significant downsides."
"Well, I'm getting withdrawal symptoms." moaned Mohammed.
"Oh, trust you!" laughed Florence.

No one noticed the bus slow down and David go to the front, looking worried. A short time passed and the bus came to a complete stop. At this point members of the group started to look up and notice that all was not well. David made a short announcement. "I'm afraid there's a road block up ahead," he said. "It may be bandits. I just need to talk to them. You must stay calm and follow the procedures I outlined yesterday."

Olly squeezed Florence's hand and she moved closer to him as a man banged aggressively on the door and shouted at David and the driver. Everyone on the bus froze and stared straight ahead at what was playing out at the front of the bus. He wore ripped and faded clothes and his leathery skin was lined and pot marked. He got very close to David's face and shouted, "Men off!" He had a large machete in his hands and he waved it at two other men outside the bus, also armed with machetes.

"Ok," said David, putting his hands up with his palms towards the bandit in order to show he didn't wish to be confrontational. "I'll get the men off the bus. The valuables are locked away but we've got money. He handed some to the bandit."

"We need to do exactly what he says," said David. "All the men need to leave the bus now but stay very close to it. Give the men outside your money. Sarah will stay on the bus with the women"

Oliver and Florence were near the back of the bus.
"I'm not leaving you," Oliver told Florence.
"Yes, you are!" said Florence, firmly. "You need to do what David says and now. Don't worry. I'll be fine."

Their conversation attracted the attention of the bandit who walked to the back of the bus. He stared at Florence and touched her hair. She winced. She could see Oliver was trying to contain himself and feared he was about to push the bandit away. He took a deep breath, glaring at the man, at which point David took his arm and guided him off the bus. Sarah moved over to the bandit and offered him her money. Florence got hers out but as she passed it to him she was aware that she was shaking violently.

The bandit moved down the bus and collected money from the women. He then got off the bus and the men started to get back on.

"Where's Olly?" asked Florence, feeling frantic. She looked out of the window just as one of the bandits pushed Oliver to ground and kicked him hard in the stomach. She cried out and David got off the bus to calm the situation. He got Oliver back on the bus and as soon as he returned the bus started to move and speed up. Oliver fought with David who was checking him for broken ribs and pushed his way back to Florence. He fell in to her arms and they held each other tight. Tears ran down Florence's cheeks and Oliver wiped them away gently.
"I thought they were going to kill you," she said.

They stopped at the next town and David rang the police who came to take statements. He gave them money to get food and drink and left Sarah to look after them. Everyone was concerned about Oliver who brushed off their concerns. "You were very brave," said Simon. "I was shaking like a leaf."

"So was I!" emphasised Oliver. "I didn't feel at all brave."
"Well you're my hero!" whispered Florence to him so no one else could hear.
"Oh, you've changed your tune Ms Bloom!" he joked with her. "It's not so long ago that you hated me!"
"Well I was wrong and I'm sorry!"
"Well, well!" he said playfully. "I bet you haven't said that very often."

"I can't wait to get my phone back, said Mohammed. My adoring fans will be worried about me and oh boy, have I got a story for them!!"

Day 94

The end was in sight. The group was enjoying their last days in a popular seaside resort with a pool. The boys had been in the pool for most of the morning playing with a beach ball and jumping in the deep end. Oliver was the only one proficient enough to dive from the top diving board and he elicited applause on a number of occasions. Mohammed's confidence had returned after his negative experience at the swimming hole and he dive bombed in to the pool in order to compete with Oliver.

The girls didn't appear until after lunch. When Florence shed her towel to reveal a bikini clad body,

Mohammed whispered, "Oh, I think I've died and gone to heaven!"
"Will you stop eyeing up my girlfriend!" laughed Oliver.
"Oh shut up!" said Mohammed. "Just appreciate how lucky you are!"
"I don't love Flo for her body. It's her sharp intellect I love her for."
"You liar!" joked Mohammed.

"Hey, Olly," shouted Florence. "Please can you come and rub sun cream in to my back?"
"I can step in there and cover for you, Mate!" joked Mohammed. "Just say the word."
"Pack it in, Mo or might decide to tell her what you've been saying and then you'll be in for a tongue lashing."
"Oh, she can lash me any time!" laughed Mohammed, closing his eyes as if imagining the scene.

Oliver walked over to Florence and rubbed her cream in and then he sat on the sun lounger next to her. "Have you had a good morning?"

Great!" she said. "I've been organising my onward travel. It would have been more exciting if it wasn't for a certain person who has put a spanner in the works!" she said, playfully, digging him in the ribs before burying herself in her book.

Oliver dozed off on the sun lounger and was woken up by a tingling sensation on his stomach. He had spots of sun cream all over it. "Have you just sprayed me with your sun cream?" he asked Florence. She ignored him and he closed his eyes again.

She left it for a while and then chanced her luck again. Without opening his eyes, he warned, "If you do that again, Madam, I'm going to chuck you in the pool."

Moments later she did it again and on this occasion, she ran for it, knowing he wouldn't tolerate her teasing any longer. She had a head start on him but he soon caught up with her and scooped her up into his arms. "Right!" he said, "You can't say you didn't ask for this." He carried her over to the pool, kicking and screaming. Instead of throwing her in, he jumped in with her. As they descended deep in to the water he noticed how her hair flowed with the water like a mermaid's and he just managed to kiss her underwater before they popped up, spluttering and screaming! He lifted her on to the side of the pool and gave her an 'I told you so!' look.
"I guess I deserved that," she said but don't think I won't get my own back!"

For most of the rest of the day, the group relaxed on sun loungers. "Oh I just love your Royal Family," said Nancy, flicking through a magazine full of glossy pictures.
"Well, you're welcome to them!" responded Florence. "I hate all that pomp and ceremony; power and privilege."

"Olly knows them all!" said Mohammed casually as Oliver gestured angrily to him to stop talking from behind Florence who was nestled in his arms on a shared sun lounger.

Florence turned to look at him and Nancy oozed, "Oh, do tell more!"

"I went to a garden party at Buckingham Palace when I was about twelve. It was an awful experience. I was forced to wear a suit and stand around for hours."

"Did you meet the queen?" asked Nancy, keen to get all the details.

"No, I just saw her from a distance. And it rained half the time so we had to endure wet and miserable weather too."

"Poor you!" said Florence, sarcastically.

"How about those gorgeous princes?" asked Nancy. "Have you met them?"

"I might have played football with them in some embassy somewhere," he said, trying to sound casual.

"OMG!" screamed Nancy. "Did you get photos? Autographs?"

"Stop it now!" ordered Florence, elbowing him in the ribs and looking at him sternly. "Nancy's going to blow a gasket if you don't!"

"So you don't want he hear about my audience with the Dalai Lama?" he whispered in her ear.

"Oh, I give up!" laughed Florence!

After dinner, Oliver pulled Florence to one side. "Keep tomorrow free because I've got a surprise organised," he told her.

"Oh, I'm intrigued," said Florence. "Do tell more!"
"No chance," he said, firmly. "Obviously it wouldn't be a surprise if I did."
"Spoil Sport! I'll ask Mo, he's bound to blab!"
"Don't think I don't know that so he knows nothing. You'd be wasting your time! We're leaving after breakfast."
"Do I need to bring anything?" she asked.
"Yes, a swimming costume."
"Ah, so it involves swimming!"
"Stop fishing because you won't get any more out of me!"

Day 95

Once breakfast was over, Oliver led Florence to the reception, still refusing to tell her anything about the day he'd planned. There they met David. "The bus is outside," he said. "Come on!"
"So where are we going then, David?" Florence asked him.
"Sorry, I've been sworn to secrecy!"
"Oh for goodness sake!" laughed Florence. "He's got all bases covered!" she said, smiling at Oliver.

It was a fifteen minute drive to the coast where they parked up in an idyllic, sandy cove.
"This is beautiful!" said Florence, delighted.
"No, we're not there yet," said Oliver.
"Aren't we?" asked Florence, confused.
"Come on, Olly, help me get the canoe off the roof."

"Canoe?"
"Yes, you see that islet just off the coast. That's where we're going!"
"Oh, wow!" exclaimed Florence. "That's idyllic! It's like something out of Robinson Crusoe."

While Oliver and David unloaded the canoe, Florence gazed at the palm fringed outcrop set like a jewel in golden sands and turquoise sea. It felt unreal.
"Right, you both need to put on these life jackets," said David. "I'll pick you up at 6 pm. Enjoy!" he said with a knowing smile.

"Right, come on you! You've got to work for your lunch!" Oliver joked, holding up a picnic basket. "Grab a paddle!"
"I don't know what to say, Olly. This is amazing."
"Something amazing for my amazing girl!"
"Stop it! You're going to make me cry!"

The islet was further than it looked and it took 30 minutes before they were paddling on to the beach. They jumped out and hauled the canoe further up the beach. They were both speechless, soaking up the atmosphere. Eventually, Oliver said, "Come on! Let's walk round the island. It won't take long!" He took her hand and they kicked off their shoes.
"I don't think I've ever been somewhere so beautiful! I bet you have."
"Maybe, but not with you so nothing compares!" he said, smiling.

They stopped half way round to collect shells. "Can you hear the sea?" said Oliver, holding up a large conch to Florence's ear.
"Yes," she laughed, and it's blowing a gale like it does back home!

They continued on and once back at the canoe, Oliver dug out two snorkels and masks. "Come on!" he said. "Let's go snorkelling!"
"Snorkelling?" said, Florence. "I've never done that before."
"It's easy," he said, fixing his mask and snorkel in place. "Come on, stay next to me. You'll love it!"

As Florence put her face under the water she felt as if she was entering another world. A kaleidoscope of colourful tropical fish of all shapes and sizes swirled and darted around below. Some were in large shoals and some looked as if they had come straight out of a fantasy world with bright and bold markings that looked unnatural to Florence's untrained eye. She had stayed close to Oliver but suddenly he dived to the sea bed below to point at colourful coral that waved in the gentle swell. As he ascended, she was amazed to spot a turtle behind him and she gestured frantically so that he turned round to see it swim past.

Once back on dry land, they lay on the sand, holding hands and gazing up at the sky. "I thought you'd spotted a shark!" Oliver joked.

"Shark? There are sharks in there?" exclaimed Florence. "Oh now you tell me!"
"Only harmless reef sharks!" he laughed. "There aren't any great whites!"
"I'm glad to hear it!" she said, smiling. "It was out of this world, Olly. Thank you!"
"It was my pleasure," he said, pulling her close. "Let's make the most of having our own desert island all to ourselves," he whispered in her ear.

After their picnic, Oliver pulled Florence to her feet. "Come on!" he said, let's climb up the hill so we can feel like King and Queen of our own castle!"

They had to fight their way through tropical vegetation but once at the top, the view across the surrounding area was stunning. "I'm going to remember this for the rest of my life!" proclaimed, Florence.
"Me too!" said Olly, kissing her.
"I wish we could stay here forever. Just you and me, alone on our desert island."
"I know," he said. "Unfortunately, I think David would send out a search party and it wouldn't be difficult to hunt us down! Come on, we'd better get going."

As they were getting back into the canoe, Florence wacked Oliver on the backside with her paddle. "Oh, you want to play dirty do you?" he laughed, grabbing her and throwing her into the sea. "Watch out for those sharks!" he shouted as he paddled off, only returning to haul her back into the canoe when she begged for mercy and apologised profusely. He spanked her playfully, in revenge, as he pulled her back on board and they collapsed in to the bottom of the canoe, giggling and kissing and letting the current take control.

David was standing on the shore tapping his watch and raising his eyebrows in disapproval when they eventually arrived back. "Sorry, David!" said Oliver, apologising profusely for several minutes. "It's all Florence's fault!"
"Well I hope you had a good time!"
"Oh, we did!" they chorused.
"And I am sorry you had to wait around but don't believe a word he says!" joked Florence.

"Get these two a Sex on the Beach," shouted Mohammed when Oliver and Florence entered the hotel bar, later that evening.
"Oh, shut up, Mo!" joked Oliver but he noticed that Florence had blushed and gone bright red.
"So how was it then?" asked Nancy. "It sounds incredibly romantic to me. Something out of a movie."
"It was wonderful!" replied Florence, recovering her composure. "Incredibly scenic."
"Oh don't try and convince us the two of you were looking at the scenery!" laughed Mohammed.
"We don't all think like you, Mo," said Oliver. "We enjoyed our snorkelling, didn't we Flo?"
"Oh, yes!" she said, "That was the best bit!"

"Oh, I give up," said Mohammed, looking exasperated. "You go to an idyllic desert island, just the two of you, and you want us to believe you spent your time looking at fish! Who are you trying to kid?"

"So who would you like to go to a desert island with then, Mo?" asked Nick. "And there are some rules, it can't be anyone who is still alive."
"You want me to go to a desert island with a dead person?" said Mohammed looking disgusted.
"No, obviously not! Just use your imagination. If you could spend time with one person in total isolation who would it be?"
"Can I have sex with them?"
"You can do whatever you like, you idiot. It's in your imagination. But we don't want all the seedy details."
"I think I'll have to think about that one. How about you, Nick?"
"Catherine the Great."
"Who?"
"Catherine the Great! She was Empress of Russia in the eighteenth century. She was a very powerful and successful woman but rather partial to younger men who she would ravish in her many opulent palaces."
"Sounds like a good candidate to me," agreed Mohammed.
"Didn't she have her husband murdered so she could seize power?" asked Oliver. "And then there's that rumour that she had sex with a horse!"
"I could overlook that," laughed Mohammed. "Ok, I've got the hang of this. Marilyn Monroe. We'd

arrive on the island, immediately strip off and go skinny dipping and then have sex on the beach for the rest of the day."

"For the rest of the day?" asked Nancy, looking incredulous.

"Yep!" replied Mohammed, "One long orgasm!"

"Ok, Nance," said Nick. "Your turn!"

Nancy thought about it for a while before responding. "The actor, Paul Newman. I love that film 'Long Hot Summer'. I've watched it over and over again. Just thinking about the scene where they kiss for the first time is making me go weak at the knees!"

"How about you, Olly?"

"Helen of Troy," he said, without hesitation. "The most beautiful woman in the world," he mused, gazing at Florence.

"Oh, someone get the sick bucket!" moaned Mohammed.

"Well I think that's beautiful, Olly!" said Fatima.

""Don't encourage him, Fatima!" scolded Mohammed. "It will just make him worse! Anyway, wasn't she a Greek myth?"

"Absolutely, too good to be true!" he said dreamily, continuing to gaze at Florence.

"You've only got yourself to blame now, Mo! Oh, and for what it's worth, can I pick a Stalin in his twenties?" said Florence.

"What?" asked the others, staring at her in bemusement."

"Well Stalin was very attractive in his twenties and I'd hope to persuade him to take a different course in life."

"Oh, yes, I see what you mean!" exclaimed Nancy, googling an image of Stalin. "Very sexy!"
"Oh, I wish I'd never started this!" groaned Nick.

"Right everyone, up on your feet!" announced Nancy, putting Abba's 'Dancing Queen' on.
"You can dance, you can jive,
having the time of your life,
Oh,Oh,Oh
See that girl, watch that scene,
dig in the dancing queen
Dig in the dancing scene"

She and Mohammed were soon up gyrating with each other and waving their arms,
"Friday night and the lights are low
Looking out for the place to go"

Fatima dragged Nick up,
"Where they play the right,
music, getting in the swing
You come in to look for a king"

and Oliver lifted Florence up in his arms and swirled her round before collapsing with her in a heap of laughter,
"You are the dancing
queen, young and
sweet, only
seventeen"

Day 96

A powerful shaft of light which magnified swirling dust in the air came through the bedroom window as Nancy styled Florence's hair in to a French plait. "Did you know there is a hot tub in the grounds of the hotel?" Nancy asked Florence.

"No!" replied Florence. "When I was at university, a friend asked a group of us to her house and she had a hot tub in the garden. We had such fun in it. It was like a different world to me."

"Do you fancy a dip in the hot tub now the sun's gone down?" asked Nancy. "It's in the gardens at the side of the hotel."

"Ok, let's go now before dinner."

As they arrived at the hot tub, Florence realised it was already occupied by Oliver, Nick and Mohammed.
"Oh!" she said, sounding rather disconcerted. "Am I the only one who didn't know about this?" she asked as Oliver enveloped her with his large frame.

"No!" he said, "Nick only told Mo and I today." The bubbles swirled round the loving couple and and Florence felt elated by the sensation of the warm frothy water and Oliver's tender embrace. She led her head on his shoulder and closed her eyes. When she opened them five minutes later, her eyes focussed on Nancy who was snuggled up to Nick. "Oh, my goodness!" she whispered to Oliver.

"What?" he asked.

"Nancy and Nick!"

"What about them?"
"Oh, open your eyes Olly!"
"I still don't get what you're getting at."
"Oh, for goodness sake! Men! Look how close they are!"
"Oh yes, now you mention it. Do you think they're in a relationship?
"Yes!"
"Well, well, well!" he smiled.

"I'm gutted!" moaned Mohammed. "Why am I the only one who hasn't got a girlfriend on this trip?"
"Don't be melodramatic, Mo! You're not the only one and you're younger than both me and Nick," said Oliver, firmly.
"You're a good looking guy, Mo. You'll get a girlfriend," Florence reassured him.
"You should be happy for Nick, Mo, Nancy's a lovely girl!" said Oliver.
"Oh yes, that reminds me of when we played Marry, Shag, Kill you wanted to marry Nancy!" said Mohammed.
"You played what?' asked Florence, looking surprised.

"Oh, thanks, Mo!" said Oliver sarcastically.
"So who did you want to shag and kill? asked Florence, rounding on him. Oh don't tell me, you wanted to kill me."
"Yep!" smiled Oliver. "But it was early days. Can you blame me?"
"More's to the point, who did you want to shag?"

"I don't remember!" he replied, coyly.
"Yes you do!" said Mohammed, enjoying Oliver's discomfort. "Jemma with the long legs!"
"Oh, thanks, Mo! Just dig my hole even deeper! You know I only have eyes for you!" he said, burying his head in her long, thick hair.

"You earnt me a right rollicking from Flo about your stupid game!" said Oliver, looking deeply unhappy.
"Sounds like fun to me!" replied Mohammed with a cheeky grin. "You should have called me! I'd have stepped in for you!"
"Oh, stop being stupid! You know what she's like. I'm really fond of her and I don't want to blow it now! She said it was a sexist game and that you'd told her I was a feminist which couldn't possibly be true if I indulged in such an immature game."
"Well trust her to bring that up! I was trying to fight your corner! You should be thanking me! I don't know why you're taking this crap from her. This all happened before you got together and, I might remind you, when she was being a right cow to you. I don't know why you don't stand up to her. You did that for a while remember, before you were all loved up."
"Um!" said Oliver, thoughtfully.
"And anyway," continued Mohammed, "I don't see her telling you to get on yer bike so what you worried about? Put your foot down! Be a man and tell her you're not going to take a lecture from her

on something that happened well before you got together."

"I'm afraid I'm not convinced that relationship counselling from you Mo is going to cement my future with Flo! I somehow think you fail to understand her psychology!"

"I helped you out when she thought you'd gone off with the gorgeous museum guide, didn't I?"

"Yes, and I'm eternally grateful, Mo but whilst you're good at chatting up women, I'm not sure your skill set runs to sustainability!"

"Well, when she's got you tied up in a basement and is starving you, don't come complaining to me!"

"Oh, stop being melodramatic! And anyway, Flo's been badly let down by the men in her life and I'm not about to be the next to let her down."

"What do you mean?" asked Mohammed.

"Oh, I've probably said too much already," said Oliver, looking awkward, but you know her dad deserted her and her mum when she was very young and well at university....."he trialed off.

"Oh!" said Mohammed. "I didn't realise."

"Please don't say anything to anyone, and certainly not Florence! I've said too much already!"

"No, of course not! I feel really bad now!"

"So you should!" smiled Oliver "But you're right, she can be a right cow!" he joked, trying to defuse the tension in the air.

Later, Oliver and Florence went for a drink in the bar.

"I'm so sorry about Mo's stupid game. I feel really bad about it and wish I'd never got involved."

"Don't worry Olly, I'm only pulling your leg. I'm sure you were just going along with Mo. I know you well enough to know you didn't invent the game!"

"Really? You mean I've spent the day worrying and you were just winding me up?"

"Yep!" she smiled, ruffling his hair.

"Mo was right! You can be a right cow!" he laughed.

"That man's a bad influence on you!"

"He told me I should put my foot down and stand up to you!"

"Oh, he did, did he?" she laughed. "You wait until I see him. I think it's about time you stopped being one of Mo's disciples!"

"Oh, you do, do you, Lady! Don't think for a minute that I'm some push over who you can tell who to be friends with!" he smiled, raising his eyebrows at her before pulling her close and holding her in a long embrace.

"I had a surprise today," said Oliver. "My parents have booked to meet up with me when we finish this trip. They're taking me to an eco-resort. I know you'll think it is a rather ponsy middle class thing to do but it does have eco in the title. A climate change activist like you has to be impressed by that. Surely."

"Oh, dear!" she said, pulling him close and whispering in his ear. "I'm clearly going to have to educate you, Mr Fraser! Next time there's a climate change protest, you won't be struggling to get across London to your wine bar, you'll be on it with me. Understood? And don't look at me like that!" she commanded, smiling.

"I think my parents thought they were going to meet you! I had to break it to them that you will have travelled on to Australia by the time they arrive! It's a shame because I want to show off my beautiful girl friend to them and my mates back home. They love the photos I've sent them. Have you told your Mum about me?"

Florence looked at the ground. "She doesn't know about the rape yet. I need to tell her about that first."

"You take your time," he said, kissing her on the head. "We've got the rest of our lives stretching out ahead of us now."

"Yes!" she said. "I feel as if I've got a future now thanks to my wonderful boyfriend." They both laughed and hugged each other.

Day 97

"When's your birthday, Mo?" asked Oliver.

"3rd October. Why?" asked Mohammed.

"Because Nick and I are going to club together to buy you a sex doll!" joked Oliver.

"It'll have to be a Pakistani sex doll to get it past my Mum. I can hardly hide it under the carpet with my porno mags!"

"Is there such a thing?" asked Oliver.

"Probably! Sounds like a great present, Guys!"

"We need to organise a boys' night out," said Mo. "How about that club in town with the posters of naked women in the window?"

"I'm fine with the night out but I'm not going to that seedy club. Let's just do a bar crawl. There are some great ones on the seafront," replied Oliver.

"Yes," said Nick, "I'm with Olly on this one."

"Oh, okay!" said Mo. "Let's put it on the Don't Tell Flossy Flo Group Chat so the other guys know about it."

"The what?" said a sharp voice from behind.

They all jumped and turned to see Florence stood behind them. "How long have you been standing there?" asked Oliver.

"Long enough," said Florence. "Now tell me about your group chat. Sounds interesting," she said, sarcastically.

"Mo was only joking but I'm afraid you're crashing a boys' meeting. Girls not welcome," said Oliver.

"You're not getting rid of me that easily, Oliver. I want to see this group chat. I don't believe you when you say it doesn't exist!"

"Look, Florence. Go and find the girls and I'll come and find you as soon as we're finished."

"No way," she said firmly.

"Right!" said Oliver, judging that his relationship with Florence could withstand drastic action. He got up and picked her up, throwing her over his shoulder. As she kicked, screamed and swore at him he mouthed "delete it" to Nick and Mohammed and carried Florence the short way down the corridor to her room. He managed to get her key out her back pocket and once he had thrown her on to her bed he moved quickly and locked her in the room.

Florence, for her part, got very angry and threatened to murder him if he didn't let her out immediately. "I'll only let you out if you calm down," he told her. "Don't patronise me!" she told him furiously.

Having figured that he had played for enough time, he unlocked the door but stood in her way. "Show me your phone!" she demanded.

Oliver wasted several more minutes looking for his phone before he told her that he must have left it on the table in the lounge. "Right!" said Florence, marching back down there and grabbing the phone off the table. "Unlock this phone and show me your group chats."

Nick and Mohammed were trying to look as if it was nothing to do with them and Oliver was praying that they had had time to delete all trace of the group chat. He unlocked it and much to his relief found that there was no trace of the offending group chat. "There you go!" he said, with an air of triumph, but inside a continuing sense of relief.
Florence eyed Nick and Mohammed, who were desperately trying to look innocent. "Oh, I get it! These two have deleted it."

"You're just paranoid, Florence," said Mohammed.
"Oh really!" said Florence.
"Well you'd better hope you got the message to all the boys to delete it before I get to them," said Florence, flouncing off.

"Oh, God!" said Mohammed. "That was close!"
"Did you get the message to all the boys to delete it?" asked Oliver, looking worried.
"I think so!" said, Mohammed. "I've had messages from everyone but Simon who's on that trip so we just need to double check with him before Florence gets to him when he returns. Can you imagine what will happen if she finds out it was us that gave her bag to that monkey."
"No!" said Oliver, "It doesn't bear thinking about! And I can tell you Mo that if she ever finds out that it was you that sent that rude picture to all her contacts, you need to tell her that I had nothing to do with that. She still thinks it was the waiter!"
"Yer, don't worry, if we all keep stum, she'll never know!"
"Mind you, let's hope she doesn't have the technical know how to know it sits in a deleted box for a month!" said Nick.
"Oh great!" said Oliver. "You mean I can't relax for a month! I'd better go and find her."

Oliver found Florence back in her room. "Can I come in?" he asked, sheepishly.
"No!" she said, angrily.

"Oh come on Flo, it was just a joke! Simon's let us have his room for the two nights he's on his trip so I'll come and get you when I get back."
"Absolutely not!" she said, looking firmly at him.
"Oh, you don't mean that!" he said, trying to sit on her bed with her and put his arm round her. "Look, I'll take you to the art galleries of Amsterdam to apologise for my dreadful behaviour," he said, edging towards her.
"Okay, but you can't bribe me" she said, still sounding suspicious, "If I ever find out you're lying to me Oliver Fraser, your life won't be worth living!"

Oliver met up with the boys at a beach bar. The music was booming and Mohammed, Nick and the rest of the group had already had a few drinks.
"So how did you get on with Flossy?" asked Mo.
"Good I think. She's suspicious but hopefully she won't dig too deep. Did you get hold of Simon?"
"Yes!" said Nick. "He's deleted it so I think we've got all bases covered."
"Thank God for that! I've been thinking about all the other things she'd find out about. That time I nicked her biscuits and Matt put vodka in her squash."
"Well, she shouldn't take herself so seriously," said Mohammed. "Can I get you a drink, Olly?"

The women met in an Indian restaurant, keen not to let the men have all the fun. They ordered an eclectic mix of exotic and spicy dishes that they shared. I think we've all got on really well on this trip, commented Fatima.

"Do you mean the girls or the whole group?" asked Nancy. "Well both really!"

"Not strictly true in my case!" joked Florence.

"No!" said Nancy, laughing. "You've gone from the sublime to the ridiculous!"

"I'd like to set you all a challenge," said Angela. One that involves winding up the boys and making them look stupid without them even knowing! Just a bit of fun!"

"Oh, I'm up for that!" said Florence, smiling. "Do tell more."

"Ok, ladies, here are your challenges and they need to take place in the lounge. I'll record your challenges beforehand and then we'll play it back to them once we've made them look foolish. Not hard with that lot!"

Florence suddenly found herself feeling defensive. Now she'd got to know Oliver she knew he was far from foolish, and neither were Nick, Mohammed and Simon but she kept quiet for fear of being called a hypocrite.

When you are carrying out your challenges, I'll try to film their reaction. So first up, my challenge. I'm going to set Mo up with a date with that sexy receptionist he's been chatting up."

"Is that safe for her?" asked Florence.

"Oh yes, she's a lesbian. She's in on it!"

"Oh my God!" said Nancy. "He' going to go mad!"

"Yes!" said, Angela and I'll be filming it!
"Jemma, you need to corner Olly and spend ten minutes talking about the weather with him."
Jemma, who was very shy, looked horrified.
"Shouldn't Florence do that?"
"Obviously not!" said Angela, looking exasperated. "That would hardly be a challenge."
"Okay, I'll try," said, Jemma, still looking very uncertain. Florence smiled at this challenge, knowing what Olly had said about Jemma's legs which were normally very much on display owing to very skimpy shorts."
Florence, you need to get Matt to gurgle his favourite football song and Fatima, you need to get Nick to talk about property law for 30 minutes. Yes, very boring, I know but that's the point."

Day 98

Florence was well hidden so she could see everything but not be seen when Jemma approached Oliver. She sat down and Florence noticed he looked very shocked and uncomfortable. When Jemma spoke to him, Florence could see he was becoming flustered. He looked at the floor but soon realised it looked as if he was looking at her legs so he looked at the ceiling. Florence left it at least ten minutes to help add to Oliver's torment. She could see he was trying to make polite conversation but he certainly wasn't relaxed. When Florence approached Oliver he looked horrified.
"Would you mind if I borrowed Olly for a moment, Jemma?"

"No, be my guest!" said Jemma, smiling knowingly at Florence.
Florence grabbed Oliver by the arm and led him to the other side of the room, close to Angela.
"What do you thing you're doing?" she asked.
Oliver looked as if he'd just been caught with his hand in a sweet jar.
"Nothing Florence, I swear! She came over to me."
"Oh, you expect me to believe that!" said Florence before flouncing out, making sure she winked at the camera before she went.

Florence managed to get Matt to gurgle his favourite football song with the added benefit that he choked and spat his drink across the room, all caught on camera by Angela. Fatima for her part got Nick sounding excited about new regulations for low carbon property.

When Angela announced that she'd managed to persuade the hotel receptionist to let them use the cinema room, Mohammed was quick to boast about the date he'd been on with the gorgeous Antonia. "She said I was the cutest guy she's been out with!"

"Oh God!" said Nick, seeing the funny side of it.
"There was me thinking you were actually interested in all that stuff!"
"Well, I'm a little bit interested, Nick but probably not to the extent that you are!" laughed Fatima.

When Oliver saw Florence wink at the camera, he dumped her off his lap and told her he would never speak to her again.
"Why are you having a go at me? What about Jemma and Ang?"
"Yes!" said Angela, "Florence had nothing to do with this challenge, Olly."
"That's not strictly true is it, Florence?" said Oliver, fixing her with a stare and refusing to let her off the hook.
Once Angela had bought everyone a drink and they started to relax, even Mohammed, who had sulked throughout the film, started to see the funny side of it.
"Simon got away with it by going on this extra excursion!" commented Mohammed.
"Oh don't worry!" his challenge is waiting for him on his return.

"Come on you," said Oliver to Florence. "Time for bed."
"I thought you weren't ever going to speak to me again," replied Florence.
"I'm going to make an exception just for tonight!"
"Oh are you?" she laughed.
"Plus, I want a word with you in private!"
When Oliver and Florence were relaxing on the bed, Oliver said, "So does Jemma know about that stupid game?"
"No!" laughed Florence and nor does Ang. It's just me that knows isn't it Olly? And you can't deny that you weren't looking at her legs!"

"I can!" he said, emphatically. "They're hard to ignore but I think I did a pretty good job. Being caught by you was a very good incentive! Now come here, I want to look at more than just your not so long but gorgeous legs!" he said.

Day 101
The group had spent several hours relaxing in the hotel bar. Most had consumed a large amount of alcohol and were enjoying relaxed conversation. Lively music was playing in the back ground and Florence, Simon and Nancy were deep in conversation about the gossip that had been generated by the long trip. Oliver, Nick, Matt and Mohammed played cards until they became too drunk to deal the cards and started to play drinking games.

A woman from reception approached with a message that Oliver took. Suddenly the mood changed as he looked horrified. "What on earth is the matter?" asked Nick.
"Oh my God!" he exclaimed. "It says your parents have arrived Mo and are in reception. They're here to surprise you!"
"Oh shit!" slurred Mohammed, looking equally horrified. "They can't see me like this! You have to cover for me guys!"
"And say what?" asked Nick.
"I don't care!" said Mohammed, starting to panic.
"They can't see me like this!" With that, he promptly fled out of the back door of the bar.

"What are we going to do now?" asked Nick.
"I'd better go and meet them!" said Oliver. "God knows what I'm going to say!"

Five minutes later Oliver returned and immediately focussed his attention on Florence. "I know it was you!" he said, narrowing his eyes and staring sternly at her.
"I don't know what you're insinuating!" she said, trying to look innocent but failing.
"Go on, admit it! The person who gave the message to reception to give to me fitted your description exactly!"
"You can't prove anything!" she said, smiling up at him.
"Watch me!" he said, also starting to lose his composure and smile.
"I'm sorry," said Nick, "but I'm confused!"
"Where are Mo's parents?" asked Nancy.
"Luton!" said Oliver. "Are you going to explain or shall I Ms Bloom?"
"Oh, ok!" said Florence. "I admit it. Revenge is a dish best served cold! I had a few scores to settle with Mo so I decided to give him the shock of his life! I got the receptionist to give Olly the message and it worked a treat!"
"Oh, I get it!" laughed Nancy. "A practical joke!"
"Nice one!" said Nick.
"Don't praise her!" smiled Oliver. "She made me look a right fool too!"

"Perhaps I had more than one score to settle!" she joked.
Oliver grabbed her and tickled her until she begged him to stop.
"So who's going to let Mo know his Mum and Dad aren't really here to check up on him?" asked Simon.
"Oh, let's have another drink first," laughed Nick.

When Mohammed emerged half an hour later he made straight for Florence and pretended to strangle her.
"You nearly gave me a heart attack," he laughed.
"And anyway what have I ever done to deserve that?"
"Oh, don't get me started!" laughed Florence. "Pole dancing, spit and swallow, sex on the beach!"
"Well if you put it like that!" he smiled.
"If I wasn't so drunk I would've realised it was highly unlikely my parents were here. They rarely leave Luton these days but when you've had a skinful you don't think straight."
Florence hugged Mohammed and offered to buy him a drink. "Well you can play practical jokes on me any time if I get to have intimate contact with you!" he joked, keeping hold of her.
"Stop encouraging him!" laughed Oliver, pulling Florence away.

"You're a very naughty girl!" whispered Oliver playfully in Florence's ear.
"I thought that was why you were attracted to me she whispered back."

"I'm attracted to your intellect and sharp wit!" he replied. "You're not going to get me like that!"

Day 102

Everyone was in buoyant mood at the final group party. Mohammed had insisted they should come in fancy dress. They kept their costumes secret until the night of the party and there was much whispering in corners as they swapped items of clothing to facilitate their costume and went off to the local shops and markets. Oliver tried to get Florence to tell him what her costume would be but she resisted, even when he held her down and tickled her until she begged for mercy. "Well, I'm not going to tell you what my costume is then," he told her.
"Fine!" she said. "I can guess! It'll be Alexander the Great or Henry VIII."
"Way off!" he joked.

On the evening, Florence and Nancy put the finishing touches to their costumes. Florence added devil's horns to her red and black costume. I think this should give some people ammunition!" she joked. "I'm looking forward to seeing what the boys are wearing!"
"Especially, Olly!" joked Nancy.

Once in the bar they spotted Mo and Nick who were dressed as Woody and Buzz Light Year. "Wow they both chimed! That's amazing!"

"Is Olly coming as Mr Potato Head?" joked Florence.
"Oy, you!" he said, coming up behind and putting his arms affectionately round her waist. She turned to see a punk rocker with spiked orange hair and Nick's leather jacket. He had a guitar to finish off the look.
"Well, I never had you down as a rebel!" she laughed.
"Just call me Sid Vicious!" he joked.

They moved towards the bar and mingled with the rest of the group. Nancy gave the long suffering DJ a list of requests and as the evening progressed the group became louder and more raucous.

Suddenly, an elegant and attractive middle aged woman appeared to complain. "Look, Guys! I really don't want to spoil your fun; I do remember what it is like to be your age but it's past 11 o'clock and my room is above."
"Oh, I'm really sorry," said Mohammed. "Can I get you a drink?"
"Oh, hello cowboy!" she said, clearly flattered by Mohammed's offer. "Mine's a gin and tonic, please."
"Follow me then," said Mohammed. "Are you on holiday?"

The others didn't see Mohammed again but noticed him dancing with the woman 30 minutes later. "The jammy devil!" said Nick.
"Don't knock it!" said Oliver. "He's kept his cougar off our backs!" They all laughed.

Shortly afterwards, Oliver pulled Florence to one side. "I'm finding you absolutely irresistible in that devil costume," he said, caressing her curves.
"Well you're going to have to control yourself!" laughed Florence.
"Not so sure about that," he said, kissing her and dangling keys in her face. "I've got Mo's keys so he won't be able to barge in on us, and anyway, I think he's occupied for a while."

Five minutes later, Oliver turned the key in the door and put on soft and sensual music. He slowly unzipped Florence's fancy dress outfit, kissing her back as he went. Florence unbuttoned his shirt and once they were both naked they showered together, letting the warm soapy water luxuriate over their entwined bodies, in a heavenly experience of arousal that they shared.

Oliver dried off and then offered his hand to help Florence out of the shower. He helped her dry off and then they reclined on the bed, kissing and caressing passionately before entering a powerful explosion of mutual sexual desire that they embraced whole heartedly.

As they relaxed together, cosy and intimate in the lamp light, there was a sharp knock on the door. "I hope you haven't fallen asleep in there, Olly!" shouted Mohammed.

"I'd completely forgotten about Mo!" laughed Oliver, passing Florence her towel in which to wrap herself. He opened the door and it was a few seconds before Mohammed noticed Florence sitting on the bed. "Oh, I get the picture!" he said with a wry smile on his face. "The shower isn't working in Florence's room so she had to come here to shower," said Oliver, trying to sound convincing.
"Do you think I fell off a Christmas tree yesterday?"
"Anyway, what have you been up to? You've been gone for a long time!" commented Oliver.
"None of your business!" he joked, "but I got her business card. Bank Manager! She says they may have an I.T. position for me!"
"Are you sure that's the only position she wants you in!" joked Oliver.
"I'm off!" said Florence. "Thanks for the use of the shower!"
"Yer, anytime!" responded Mohammed. "Pop round when Olly's not here next time and I can show you the power shower and body jet settings! I'll make sure it's hot and steamy for you! I can guarantee a wet and wild experience!" he said, grinning at Oliver who was glaring at him.

Day 103

Fatima and Florence arranged to have a coffee together, aware that their time together was coming to an end. "You've been an inspiration to me," Fatima told Florence.

"Have I?" asked Florence, looking surprised.
"Yes, you've really changed your mind set on this trip. You've made a conscious decision not to let your past damage your future and I really admire you for that. I'm going to take a leaf out of your book and do the same myself. I've decided that when I get home, I'm going to foster children."
"That's great news, Fatima! Good for you! You'll make a great foster Mum. I know because you've been like a foster Mum to me on this trip," said, Florence.
They had a hug and shed some tears.
"I've got you this," said Florence. "Just a small token of my thanks for all your support."
"Oh, Florence! I didn't expect this," she said, opening the present. "Oh, that's beautiful! It's one of those candles we were admiring at the market. I love it! Come here!" she said, kissing and hugging Florence.
"You have to read the quote in the card to understand why I bought you the candle," urged Florence.
"Ok," said Fatima, opening the card. "*'How far that little candle throws its beams! So shines a good deed in a naughty world.' Portia, Merchant of Venice.* Oh you're going to make me cry again!"
"We must stay in touch!" said Florence.
"Absolutely!" agreed Fatima.

"I can't believe it's our last night after all these months of travel," said Mohammed. "I'll be glad to get back to some home comforts but I'm going to miss you guys."

"Yes, I know what you mean!" said Oliver, thoughtfully. "I didn't expect to become so close to everyone."
"Yes, and one person in particular!"
"You're right! That one came right out of the blue! At the start I thought she might murder me in my sleep!"
"Well, good job she's changed her tune because I've arranged to bunk up with Simon tonight so you two can have the room all to yourselves for the whole night."
"I don't know what to say, brother. I love you!"
"Did you call me brother?"
"Yes, Mo. I don't know what I would have done without you at times on this trip."
"I love you too, bro. And I'm up for being your best man!"
"I think you're jumping the gun but you're top of the list!"
"Dave is going to arrange free drinks for us all after 'the incident' and Nick, your solicitor, has insisted you get champagne brought to the room! I think the company is scared he's going to sue them on our behalf!
"I'm going to make myself scarce. Nancy is going to make sure Flo gets here in time to watch the sunset so you'd better get yourself spruced up. Slap on the after shave!"
"Thanks again, Mate!"

One hour later, there was a knock on the door. "Hello, gorgeous!" said Oliver. "You look stunning." She had borrowed a cocktail dress from one of the other girls and wore her hair up for the first time. He pulled her in to the room and kissed her. "How am I going to let you go to Australia?"

The bottle of champagne was on the balcony table with two champagne glasses and when the cork popped they drank to their relationship. "How did we ever get together?" mused Florence. "I remember taking an instant dislike to you on day one," she joked.
"I don't think I even noticed you until a few weeks in!"
"Really?" she asked, looking hurt.
"No, of course not! I fell for you the second I set eyes on you! I was just petrified of you! I still haven't got over the telling off you gave me after Mo jumped in to that swimming hole!"
"Don't remind me!" she said, wincing.
"Do you remember pushing me over?" he asked.
"Oh God, yes!" she said. Putting her head in her hands. "I'm really sorry about that."
"No, it's me who should apologise. I was trying to wind you up when you were in a vulnerable position. I should have waited until I broached the whole thing about Cambridge University."
"I didn't drink a drop after I was raped until that night. I'd had a few drinks when I was attacked and I still feel as if I made myself unnecessarily vulnerable. I guess it suggests I was starting to heal when I enjoyed drinking on our night out but I just didn't realise what sort of affect it would have on me."

"Please don't say you made yourself vulnerable. You have every right to drink alcohol and not be violated in that way. Even if you'd been blind drunk, which you clearly weren't, he had no right to do that and should be rotting in jail as we speak."

"Thanks, Olly! I don't think anyone had ever said no to him. His family is very wealthy and I think he thought I was just another woman who would do his bidding like the cleaners and secretaries who work for his family."

"We had staff abroad but it was always made clear to me that they weren't there to clean up after me and I would have been in big trouble if I had ever shown any kind of disrespect to anyone."

"Well, therein lies the difference," said Florence. "Something that it took me a while to realise!"

They fell in to silence before Oliver said, "Mind you! You can be a really snotty cow at times!" he laughed, picking her up and throwing her on the bed where he silenced her protests by kissing her so passionately that she couldn't speak.

After finishing the champagne, Florence took out a small wrapped package and handed it to him. This is for us to share. He unwrapped it and pulled out two interconnected necklaces. "Read the card that goes with it," said Florence.

'Yin and Yang

In Ancient Chinese philosophy, yin and yang is a concept of dualism, describing how seemingly opposite or contrary forces may actually be complementary, interconnected, and interdependent in the natural world, and how they may give rise to each other as they interrelate to one another.'

"I don't know what to say!" he said, starting to cry. That's us!"
They each put on one of the necklaces. "Come here," he said, hugging her close.

"I've got this for you," said Olly, handing her a small wrapped package. "It's a guardian angel to tie on to your ruck sack for when you're in Australia. Think of it as me watching over you."
"Oh, Olly!" she said, "that's such a lovely idea!"

They watched the sun slip down over the sea and reminisced about their adventures.

Day 104
When they woke up in each other's arms the next morning, Oliver brushed Florence's hair out of her eyes. "This isn't going to be just a holiday romance, is it?"
"Not if I have anything to do with it," she said. "I never thought I could have a loving relationship after I was raped but you've proved me wrong."
"I'd like to kill him for doing that to you," Oliver said angrily.

"I feel sorry for him. He'll never, ever have what we have. Something very precious."
Oliver looked distressed. "I've just realised that Henry will never have what I have."
"No, you're right," Florence said, stroking his hair, "and that is very hard but knowing you as I do, I know he wouldn't want you to be unhappy for the rest of your life."

Florence looked at her watch and suddenly realised the time. We need to get breakfast because I have a bus to the airport to catch. Thank goodness I packed yesterday.

After breakfast, Oliver, Mohammed, Nick, Nancy, Fatima and Simon accompanied Florence to the bus station. After lots of hugs, kisses and promises to keep in touch Oliver pulled Florence to one side. "I'm going to miss you!" he said. "You know I'd go to the ends of the earth for you! I could come and meet you in Australia at some point," he mused, hugging her tight. "Wow! That sounds like a plan!" said Florence, excitedly. He pushed a carrier bag in to her hand and she peered inside. It was the t-shirt he'd lent to Nancy. "It even still smells of me I'm afraid, I didn't get round to washing it," he said, kissing her. "Perfect!" laughed Florence.

The bus spluttered in to life and she had to run to catch it. It was gone in an instant and a plume of exhaust fumes.

As Oliver stood alone, not sure what to do next, his phoned pinged. "I love you!"
He messaged back, "I love you too!"

Printed in Great Britain
by Amazon